Obsession

EXPLICITLY YOURS ◆ BOOK FOUR

JESSICA HAWKINS

© 2015 JESSICA HAWKINS
www.JESSICAHAWKINS.net

Editing by Elizabeth London Editing
Proofreading by Tracy Seybold
Cover Design © OkayCreations.
Cover Photo © shutterstock.com/g/kiuikson

Obsession (EXPLICITLY YOURS SERIES 4)

This book is a work of fiction. Names, characters,
places, and incidents either are products of the
author's imagination or are used fictitiously. Any
resemblance to actual persons, living or dead,
events, or locales is entirely coincidental.

ISBN: 0-9978691-4-3
ISBN-13: 978-0-9978691-4-9

TITLES BY
JESSICA HAWKINS

LEARN MORE AT JESSICAHAWKINS.NET/BOOKS

SLIP OF THE TONGUE
THE FIRST TASTE
YOURS TO BARE

THE CITYSCAPE SERIES
COME UNDONE
COME ALIVE
COME TOGETHER

EXPLICITLY YOURS SERIES
POSSESSION
DOMINATION
PROVOCATION
OBSESSION

STRICTLY OFF LIMITS

Chapter One

Lola drove straight through the heart of night, her only company the stars and the Lotus Evora's hum, which she preferred to the radio. Not even the moon showed its scarred face. She straddled her past and her future, unstuck but not quite free. She refused to think too hard of *him* until she was far enough away that she couldn't turn back.

Her plan had played out even better than she'd thought, except that she'd expected to feel more vindicated by now. It was still early, though. Not even the sun had risen since she'd left Beau at Cat Shoppe, pacing out front, waiting for her to emerge. How long had it taken him to realize she never would?

When her fuel tank neared empty, she finally loosened her grip on the steering wheel and pulled off the freeway. She found a gas station and, once inside, did a quick scan of the building—a side effect from the time she'd walked in on Beau with a gun to his head.

The clerk stared openly at her chest. "Nice car."

Lola closed the top button of her coat. She slapped cash on the counter, making him jump. "Pump five, a pack of Marlboros, a lighter and coffee."

"Sure thing, babe." He took the money.

Night fringed and frayed into dawn. She set the tank to fill and leaned against a wall to smoke. Her shiny, spotless new Lotus held two duffel bags—one had her personal things, and the other, stashed in the trunk, held what was left of her million dollars. All that money, right there, made her head swim. She tapped ash from her cigarette and glanced over her shoulder. The clerk was watching her through the window.

She was on her own now. With Johnny and Beau, she'd always had someone behind her. Tonight, her back was up against the wall, and everything she owned in the world was right in front of her. One twist of fate, one slip up, and she could lose it all. An accident. A thief.

Beau Olivier.

He would come after her, at least at first. She had to watch her every move—not even a footprint in the sand he could track. Because if he caught her, there was no telling what he'd do to her for this. For tricking him into loving her and making him a fool ten times greater than she had the first time.

Lola didn't want to think about that. It was a happy night. She stubbed out her cigarette and got back in the car. She'd already scarfed her beef Pad Thai and steamed vegetables somewhere around Bakersfield. Gas and coffee would buy her a few more hours until she needed to crash. She debated going back in for a candy bar, but she wasn't as far as she wanted to be yet, so she started the car instead.

She drove straight to the next biggest city. Night and day wrestled as the sun woke up over California. Lola put on her oversized, designer sunglasses, one of the few things left from her life with Beau, and relaxed back into her seat. As San Francisco's skyline came into view, she thought—*so this is it. This is my freedom, my revenge.*

She watched out the windshield as she passed the St. Regis hotel, glimpsing its swank interior through tall windows. Lola was flush now, but she was heading into an uncertain future. She had to be careful with what she had, and she'd already spent a good chunk on the Lotus, a gift to herself.

Motel 6 was more her speed anyway, and she'd already made a reservation. She'd be comfortable there. She paid for the room in cash and drove around back. After shutting off the car, she sat a minute, checking the parking lot and then all her mirrors.

Far as she could tell, no one was around. She got her things, popped the trunk for the bag of money and carried everything to the room. Inside, she went directly to the closet. Every Motel 6 was supposed to have a safe—but she slid open the door and found nothing.

The cash weighed heavily on her shoulder. Lola dropped it on the bed, picked up the phone and hit a button.

"Front desk," a man answered.

"I need a new room. I'm in 103."

"Is there an issue?"

"This one faces the parking lot." Lola sniffed. She wasn't about to advertise how badly she needed a safe. "I want to be near the pool."

"Hang on." The line went quiet a moment, and then he said, "Nothing open by the pool."

"Maybe I should go somewhere else then."

"Um…" His voice trailed off jaggedly, a froggy sound. "Want me to suggest another hotel in the area?"

Lola sighed. Threatening to take her business elsewhere didn't quite have the same effect as when Beau did it. "No. Is there anything else available?"

"Yes, ma'am. Just not by the pool."

"Whatever. Any other room is fine."

Lola picked up the duffel again, put it back in her trunk and drove around to the front desk. She locked the car, exchanged the key and parked where she'd be able to see the Lotus from her window. This room had a safe, but it wasn't big enough for her bag. She took out stacks of cash, fitting as much in as she possibly could and put the rest under the mattress. She'd also stuffed a small amount into the spare tire compartment of the car. Diversifying your wealth was important. Or so she'd heard.

When she'd gotten the rest of her things, she closed the blinds, bolted the door and crawled under the covers. Thanks to Beau, she'd developed quite the habit of going to bed *after* the sun came up.

Lola closed her eyes, exhausted from the last twenty-four hours. So much had gone down, but she didn't want to think about any of it. She just wanted to sleep. Her immediate plan had been to get as far as she could in a small amount of time. Now, the whole country was open to her. She had no obligations—no other reservations or arrangements. She'd worry about that when she woke up, though.

Lola turned onto her side and pulled a pillow between her arms. Sleeping next to Beau had never been hard. He usually was out a few seconds after he closed his eyes, and then she could relax in his presence and enjoy the way he held her—protectively, like someone might try to take her in the middle of the night.

His waking moments, though—they'd given her some trouble. The past three weeks, Lola had tried not to think too hard about abandoning her plan and staying with Beau. The temptation had been too dangerous then. But what was the harm in it now?

Things had been far from perfect between them. Beau'd claimed to know her inside out, but he hadn't even realized how empty her days had been. He'd bungled little things, like buying her a peach dress for the ballet when it was the last color she would've picked for herself. He'd fucked up the big things too, though, like thinking she could be content just to be by his side—no job, no life of her own. Just her, at his beck and call.

Lola sighed, hugging the pillow more tightly. The night they'd discussed her getting a job was one she remembered well. It'd almost been a turning point for them. If Beau had done and said all the right things, would she still be here now, sleeping without him?

Alone, in the darkened room, without a steel cage around her heart for the first time in weeks, she let herself go there.

Chapter Two

One week earlier

Lola didn't look up from her plate when Beau entered the kitchen. He was late. She didn't actually care—presuming he might miss dinner again, she'd eaten without him—but that wasn't how a woman in love acted. So she'd made herself a new plate of food and read a magazine until the garage door rumbled open.

"I left work as soon as I could." Beau loosened his tie and opened the refrigerator to grab a beer. In Beau's world, that was as close to an apology as she was going to get.

"You said you'd be home three hours ago." Lola stood, picked up his plate and walked over to him. She shoved it between them, steamed carrots rolling off onto the floor. "Is this how it's going to be? After everything we went through, work's always going to come before me?"

"No." He took the plate from her and set it on the counter. "Of course not."

"This isn't what I signed up for."

"And it's not what you're getting. You have no idea the day I've had. I'm not even hungry. All day, I just wanted to come home and," he put his knuckle under her jaw, "and...kiss you."

Lola parted her lips but turned her head away when he leaned in. The argument wasn't over. Night after night, she sat by herself, waiting for him to come home. She hadn't given up her comfortable life to live unhappily in second place. "You're supposed to be making some changes."

He guided her face back to his. "I know what I said, and I'm trying. There's going to be an adjustment period, Lola. I can't suddenly start leaving the office at five when I normally work twelve-hour days." He touched his thumb to the corner of her mouth. "As much as I want to get home to you, I have to ease into this."

"I know," she said. He looked like he was going to kiss her. She salivated. Not every part of her could be schooled. "I just thought we'd get more time with each other. I'm used to having someone around. Johnny and I were together morning, noon and—"

"Don't." Beau pinned her with a look and dropped his hand. He inhaled through his nose. "Get mad at me if you want, but don't bring him up. That's the last fucking thing I want to hear after a long day."

"You're right. I'm sorry." Johnny was a weapon that never lost its potency. It had as much effect on

Beau now as it had their first night together when he'd lost his cool and fucked her up against the hotel window. Lola shivered at the memory and slid her arms up around his neck. "Ready for that kiss?"

He hummed a noise of approval. She rose onto the balls of her feet, threading her fingers in his hair, bringing his lips down to hers.

"This right here," he said, "may be the greatest threat to my work. How am I supposed to focus knowing you're here waiting for me each night?"

"That's all I want," she whispered. She rested her forehead against his and opened a vein. It was necessary, sometimes, to tell the truth in order to draw him in. To feel the things she tried not to. "To be enough for you to leave work early."

"You are. I'm not the kind of man who leaves work early, though, and you knew that. I love what I do, even more so now, because it enables me to give you what you want."

"But...you're what I want. Not clothing or parties or cars. I want time, and I want it with you."

He pulled her closer by the small of her back so they were flush against each other. "You make an excellent case," he whispered in her ear, as if someone might hear. "Let me make it up to you."

She shook her head. "Not yet."

"That's not what I'm getting at. Tonight, I'm all yours. I'll shut off my phone, and we can talk and catch up. All night long, if that's what it takes."

Lola pulled back a little. "But you have to work in the morning."

"Don't worry about that. I've done it before, if you recall."

Lola narrowed her eyes. The corner of her lip twitched. "Aren't you getting a little old to pull so many all-nighters?"

He laughed, slapping her rear end lightly. "Sounds like you don't think I can do it. Is that a challenge, Miss Winters?" He released her and walked away, disappearing into the pantry.

She gave in to her smile. "Does that always work on you?"

"What?" he called.

"Well, for example—if I were to tell you I don't believe you can do laundry, would you do it just to prove me wrong?"

"I do laundry just fine." Beau came out with a bag of ground beans. "I'm going to put a pot on. Let's move this to the couch."

Lola took the coffee from him. "I'll make this. I'm sure you're dying to get out of your suit."

He kissed her quickly on the lips and brushed a lock of her hair from her forehead. "Have I said how much I love having you around to take care of me?"

Lola caught herself grinning after he'd left the kitchen and quickly wiped the smile from her face. She had an entire, uninterrupted night to worm her way into his heart. And he wasn't going to lay a hand on her. For as obstinate as he could be, Beau wasn't as difficult to move around the playing board as she would've thought.

Once the coffee was ready, she poured two mugs and met Beau in his den. It was the only room besides his that was remotely comfortable, and while he rarely spent any time in there, she frequently did.

Lola sat beside him on the couch and handed him his drink. He clinked his mug with hers. "To keeping my dick in my pants another night—Lord knows it isn't easy."

She laughed and pushed his shoulder. "I'm not drinking to that."

"All right." He winked. "To quality time."

They both took a sip, and she set her cup on the coffee table. She scooted closer to him and ran her fingers over his hairline, just above his ear. "So, why was it such a long day?"

"I don't want to talk about work." He readjusted to face her better. "What'd you do today?"

"Slept in."

He raised his eyebrows at her. "You don't say. Then what?"

"I read the newspaper. Looked up some stuff online. Before I knew it, it was almost time to start dinner, so I went grocery shopping."

"Sounds nice." He cleared his throat and rubbed her knee. "It makes me happy that you don't have to work. But have you thought about doing something more...um—doing something else with your free time?"

Lola rolled her lips together. Of course she'd thought about it. She was bored all the fucking time wandering around this shell he called a home or going shopping for things she knew she'd have to leave behind. She wanted a job, and not just because she knew a million dollars wouldn't last forever. But there was no point in getting one when she was leaving soon.

"I've thought about it a little," Lola said. "It's just so nice not to have to bust my ass cleaning up after drunk idiots anymore."

"You were wasting your potential at Hey Joe. I knew it the minute I walked into that dump."

She cocked her head. "But I have no other skills."

"Go back to school." His eyes lit up, and he shifted his body even more toward her. "I have connections at UCLA and USC. It wouldn't be a problem to set you up there."

Lola felt a little like moving away from him, but she stayed where she was. It was Beau's kneejerk response to any problem—how could his money and status solve it so he didn't have to?

"I suppose you'd also be willing to pay my way," she said.

"Why wouldn't I?" He shrugged. "Look, I'd have absolutely no problem with you staying home every day and doing nothing if I thought it'd make you happy. Plenty of guys I know have wives who do that and go to expensive luncheons every month so they can call themselves philanthropists." He sipped his coffee. "That's not you, though. You can do whatever you want now. You never let yourself have dreams and aspirations before, but there's nothing holding you back anymore."

Lola also picked up her mug and took a drink, hiding her face for a moment. If he kept pushing her, everything she'd been thinking lately might come pouring out. There were lots of things she wanted to do, and going back to school was one of them. She'd been debating between majoring in graphic design or business. Maybe both. She wasn't limited—she could be a goddamn mechanic if she wanted. But she wasn't focusing on herself yet. It was Beau's time in the spotlight.

She changed the subject. "What if there're other things I want to do first?"

Beau settled back, crossing his arms. "Such as?"

"I want to travel. I've never been past Vegas."

Beau nodded approvingly. "Where should we go? Paris? Bali? New York City?"

She hadn't lied earlier—she really had spent a good portion of her day kicking back, researching things to do around the country. "That's a little ambitious. Did you know the world's largest ball of twine is right here in the United States?"

"It's nothing to write home about."

She smirked. "You haven't seen it."

"You're right, I haven't. Big balls don't do anything for me. But if they impress you, I can show you a couple—"

"Don't even." Lola rolled her eyes, grinning.

"You have the whole world to choose from, and you pick—where'd you say this ball was?"

"Kansas. Where would you go if you were me?"

"I've been a lot of places. For me, it's less about what I'm seeing than how it makes me feel."

"So what's made you feel?"

13

"Hard to say. There's so much to choose from." Beau blinked away, drank a little coffee. He looked into his mug.

Lola studied him. He seemed to forget she was there for a moment. "What are you thinking about?" she asked.

He glanced up. "The last trip we took as a family before my dad died was the Grand Canyon. Standing there, the world seemed so big. So many possibilities. It was the first time I started to think I could do something with my life. If there were things out there like the Grand Canyon I still didn't know existed, then there must be a way for me to find them."

"Always so serious," Lola murmured. She laced her fingers with his. If she ever came across a little boy like the one Beau had been, she vowed to buy him an ice cream or tell him a dirty joke. There were consequences to taking oneself so seriously. "Have you been back?"

"Yes." He glanced down at their hands. "After I sold my first company, the same night I met you, I doubted myself. I wasn't sure which way to turn. I drove to Arizona and looked out at the Grand Canyon, waiting for answers. A place like that really makes you realize how little control you have. But it also puts things in perspective."

"I get the feeling keeping perspective hasn't really been an issue for you."

"Not usually. It helps to separate emotion from most things." Beau took Lola's mug from her, set their drinks on the coffee table and looked at her. "Don't think I don't realize how lucky I am. I almost lost you because of pride, but you gave me a second chance and saved me from a lifetime of regret."

Lola let herself get lost in the comforting green of his eyes. Tonight, she was one half of a normal couple. How could Beau not see right through her? Hear the undercurrent of her distrust in everything she said? *She* was the one left with regret—regret that he'd made her do this. And that she'd never get to witness his suffering.

He leaned in to touch his lips to the bow of hers and made his way around her mouth with light, gentle kisses. She could've told him right then that she loved him, and it wouldn't be a lie. But the closer they got to the end, and to each other, the more afraid she became that saying it aloud would feel too good.

His hands were on her cheeks now. His patience unnerved her. "I'm hungry, Lola," he said so softly, she almost missed it.

"I'll heat up your dinner." She went to pull away, but he kept her there.

"Not for food." He ran the pad of his thumb along her bottom lip. "I want to know you inside out. And for you to want the same from me."

"I do."

"Do you?"

"It's not a race, Beau. Be patient."

"I am. We have all night."

That was almost true. Lola wasn't sure who fell asleep first, just that it happened sometime before the sun came up, after they'd talked and talked about everything and nothing in particular.

15

Around dawn, Beau stirred. Lola squeezed him closer with her arm, not ready to lose his warmth. "Stay," she murmured.

"It's almost six."

"Take the day off."

He kissed the top of her head and raked his fingers through her hair. "I can't. Not right now."

Lola sighed deeply. She was already drifting back to sleep when he moved her arms and shifted her aside so he could stand.

"Want me to take you upstairs?" he asked.

"I'm fine here." Her eyes were still closed. She felt around for a pillow to take Beau's place, yawned and burrowed into it. "Have a good day, honey."

The room was quiet a moment, and she assumed he'd left. Then he said, "You've never called me by anything other than my name."

It took her a moment to realize she wasn't dreaming. Lola blinked her eyes open. She got up on an elbow and squinted at him. "What? What'd I call you?"

"Honey."

Beau's hair stuck up on one side from sleeping against the arm of the couch, and his eyelids were heavy. Light was just beginning to filter through the blinds. Lola couldn't remember how she'd gotten there and what she was supposed to be doing.

Beau came back to the couch and squatted to kiss her on the forehead. "It's nice waking up with you. My day can only go downhill from here."

He stood, but Lola grabbed his arm. "Then stay with me."

16

He brought her hand to his mouth and kissed it. "Call me when you get up. We can get lunch."

He let go and left the den. Lola rubbed her eyes and watched through the door as he climbed the stairs toward his bedroom. It'd been a nice moment, but it was cut short by Beau's devotion to the only thing that had his loyalty—his work. Business. The empire he looked down upon from his office in the sky.

And then Lola remembered where she was and how she'd gotten there.

Chapter Three

Present day

Twelve hours, thirty-one minutes, eleven seconds. That was how much time had passed since Beau'd hung up the phone with Detective Bragg. Lola had been missing even longer. She wasn't missing, though. She was just gone. Beau couldn't wrap his head around how easily she'd erased herself from his life. Between disappearing without a trace and Brigitte cleaning out Lola's things, it was as if she'd never even been there. She had, though, and once he found her, this uneasy feeling she'd left him with would finally go away.

Beau rubbed his eyes with tense fingers, the air in his office stale. She'd told him once she'd never been past Vegas. There was a whole fuck-of-a-lot beyond that. Every minute that went by, she got farther away from him. He wouldn't even entertain the notion that her first stop might've been LAX airport—he couldn't take on the rest of the world right then.

Beau finally got some relief when his cell vibrated on his desk, Bragg's name popping up. He answered it. "How far did she get?"

"I got nothing."

Beau's grip tightened. He didn't have the brain capacity to accept that Bragg might fail him. Bragg was a go-to man, someone who'd made a decent living making things happen. "I'm sorry, can you repeat that? I thought you said you have nothing."

"It's what I said. Went to Cat Shoppe last night and talked to Kincaid, the owner. After a chunk of cash that I'm tacking onto your bill, I finally got him to show me the surveillance tape. That's some show your girl put on for you."

Beau's gut smarted as though he'd been punched. "You watched?"

"Don't get shy on me, Olivier." Bragg chuckled into the phone. "That's what you wanted, isn't it? Leave no stone unturned? I see what the fuss is about, though."

"Get to the point." It'd been his last intimate moment with Lola, her dancing on stage just for him, but now two greasy old men had shared in it too. That was the fucking goodbye gift Lola had given him.

"After security removed you, Lola talked to a girl, but she swears up and down Lola didn't tell her nothing. Just needed help getting the backdoor open."

"So she walked out the back. Then what?"

"Some brief indistinguishable activity by your car and then poof. Gone."

"What, in a car? Bicycle? Come on, Bragg—this is rookie shit."

"It look to you like I got a crystal fucking ball? I only see as far as the camera does, and it stops in the parking lot."

"What about the owner? What's he know?"

"Said she used to work for him, and she stopped by earlier that day to arrange the VIP room. Paid him a lot in cash. That was all he'd give me. Not sure if he knows more—bouncer said he's protective of his girls."

Beau leaned his knuckles on his desk. "I got the same thing from him."

"Only reason he showed me the tapes was because I threatened to get the police involved. Didn't seem too bothered about it until I flashed my old badge."

Lola was too good. She must've considered Beau might go after her, and she hadn't left him any obvious clues except the ones on his car. He pushed off his desk and turned to look out the window. "What about Hey Joe?"

"Yeah. Bit of a confrontation there. You spoke to Veronica?"

"Lola's friend."

"Says she hasn't spoken to Lola since she left Hey Joe, and I believe her. But the ex-boyfriend and his new girlfriend really don't like me there—he starts pushing my buttons."

Beau cocked his head. "His girlfriend?"

"Skanky thing."

21

"Amanda?"

"Yeah, that's her. Her lip curls just hearing Lola's name. Anyway, I had to rough Johnny up a little."

Beau had been picturing Lola's reaction to hearing Johnny and Amanda were still together, but that got his attention. "You *what?*"

"I may be getting up there, but I got almost fifty years of training behind me," he said defensively. "The kid tested my reflexes and got a surprise. He'll be all right—nothing a towel of ice and a blowie from the skank won't take care of." Bragg coughed into the phone. "Next stop is the diner to see the mom."

Beau didn't have any sympathy for Johnny. He had it coming. But he had no idea what they were in for with Lola's mom since he knew little about her. Suddenly, it didn't feel right sending a stranger to her workplace. "Forget the mom," Beau said. "What about the airport? Her credit cards?"

"Nothing and nothing."

Beau paused. "Nothing—as in, you haven't gotten to it yet?"

"No activity on the card you gave her. I assumed you canceled it."

"No." It hadn't occurred to him that he should, and he wouldn't now that she didn't have a cell phone or credit card he knew of. It was stupid of her, and she wasn't stupid. You didn't grow up how they did and not look out for yourself. She was her own responsibility, she'd made that clear, but Beau couldn't help thinking of the trouble she might run into.

"You ought to think about it," Bragg said.

"What?"

"You know, canceling any other cards she might've stolen. Checking to see if you're missing anything of value—jewelry, cash, art…"

Beau shook his head. "This isn't about money. You tried seeing if she opened a new card?"

"Can't find nothing under her name."

"Try Jonathan Pace."

"Already did. She had a card with him, but it was canceled a few weeks ago too. You said it was stolen, right?"

Beau tapped a finger on his desk. Lola'd told him she'd ordered herself a backup credit card in addition to what he'd given her. He should've insisted on seeing it, but he'd been happy enough that she'd agreed to stop spending her own money.

"Don't worry," Bragg said. "She's got to be paying for stuff somehow."

Beau's heart thudded once. He didn't know if Lola had a cell phone or credit cards. He didn't know how she was traveling or where. The only thing he knew for sure was that she had cash. Cash *he'd* given her. "She has money," Beau said quietly.

"She'd need a hell of a lot to stay off the grid much longer, though."

Beau closed his eyes. There it was, the cherry on top of this shit sundae. The final nail in his coffin—and he'd hammered it in. "She has more than a lot."

"Yeah? Well, cash is a different beast, Olivier. How'm I supposed to find someone who's gone out of her way not to leave a trail?"

"I don't know. I hired you to figure that stuff out." Beau's mouth was as dry as a cotton ball. Pieces of the puzzle were falling into place, and the blame was coming down on his shoulders. "Don't tell me this is impossible, Bragg. I need you on this."

Bragg sighed. "Someone's got to talk to the mom. Clock's ticking."

The line went dead. Beau had always known exactly where to find Lola if he needed her—Hey Joe, her apartment, the Four Seasons, and then, his own home. It was a luxury he hadn't realized he'd been afforded. Now, it'd been yanked away.

Lola had disappeared without a trace and left no sign she was coming back. That was what his money had bought her.

◆ ◆ ◆

Beau boarded the elevator. He needed to get out of the office and away from the people he saw day in and day out. After Bragg's useless phone call, he only had more questions. When he'd sold his first company and found himself unsure of which way to turn next, he'd gone to the Grand Canyon. But he had a meeting in forty-five minutes he couldn't miss, so he'd have to find another way to get some perspective.

He stopped at the coffee stand in the lobby. Bolt Ventures had moved into the top two floors of this downtown Los Angeles skyscraper nearly ten years ago, yet he couldn't recall ever having ordered anything from the little shop near the building's entrance. His assistant always had a pot waiting when he arrived for the day.

"Black coffee," he told the girl behind the counter.

She entered his order into the register. "Two seventy-five."

"For a small?"

"There's only one size."

Beau raised both eyebrows at her before peeling some ones from his wallet. Three dollars for coffee was painful. He took no issue with splurging on certain things—a glass of Glenlivet or a bespoke suit—but those tastes had taken time to cultivate. He'd been raised frugal. A three-hundred-something-percent markup didn't sit right with him.

Beau took his drink outside to walk around the block—another thing he'd only done a handful of times. He didn't recognize half the shops. The sidewalk seemed more crowded than the last time he'd been out there in the middle of the day without a car.

He'd spared no expense for Lola. She was the smooth and supple whisky, the Merino wool with price tags he hadn't batted an eyelash at. His bank account was considerably lighter for having known her—mostly from what he'd spent for two nights with her—but there was the extended hotel stay, gifts, room service, shopping that'd come with it. He didn't mind. He'd rather have spent his money on her than himself. Though there were days he'd wanted to leave work early to be with her, he'd reminded himself that his success was dependent on the time he put in each day. It belonged to her too, his success. Or, it had. Now, he questioned all those hours he'd been at the office instead of home with her. Would it have changed anything?

Beau'd been walking blindly, ignoring his surroundings, until a dark-haired woman twenty feet in front of him caught his eye. Despite it being a weekday, and a cool one at that, she wore a gold, floor-length gown that elongated a tan, smooth back. Just like the tan, smooth back he'd recently worshipped. Just like the gold, shimmering dress he'd ruined their second night together.

Beau tossed his coffee in the nearest trash and picked up his pace. Lola was playing a game with him. She could show up just as suddenly as she'd disappeared. Was she so brave to come to his office? Nobody just picked up and left the way she had— without a plan, without anything but a bunch of cash.

He flexed his hand with the urge to grab her elbow, yank her through the nearest door and take her up against a wall before she could even explain herself. She'd wreaked havoc on his life. She'd used sex as a weapon to keep him distracted. Anger and need surged through him.

She turned a corner. He broke into a jog, weaving through the crowd of tourists and businesspeople. He rounded the block and stopped short to avoid stumbling over a large orange cone.

A short man in a headset stepped into his path. "You have to go around. Street's closed for a photo shoot."

The woman stood in the center of an empty, blocked-off road, surrounded by a team of people dressed in black. She turned and caught Beau staring at her. Her midnight-colored hair shone in the sun, and she shimmered in liquid gold. She wasn't Lola.

"Hello?" The man waved his clipboard. "You can't get through here."

Beau backed away, keeping his eyes on her. A man in a tuxedo joined her in the street.

"Put your arms around her," a photographer said, his camera aimed at them.

The male model took her by the waist, and she lifted her face to his.

"Don't let him kiss you. Make him work for it."

She put her palm on his chest, and he leaned in, but she stayed just outside his reach. The camera snapped over and over. Right before Beau turned away, the woman glanced over at him and, he could've sworn—smirked.

Chapter Four

Lola strained to see out the passenger's side window. Nothing could've prepared her for the grandeur of the Golden Gate Bridge or the view it gave her of San Francisco. She'd spent the evening before walking around the city without seeing the same thing twice— and now, for these few seconds, she could see the entire place all at once.

She took her camera from her purse, snapped a one-handed picture out the window and put it away. She put *San Francisco* away—it was time to move on after only one night. Beau would be looking for her by now, and she couldn't stay anywhere too long.

Once she was on the freeway, she checked her rearview mirror and then the speedometer. The needle hovered at seventy miles per hour. It was a crime to finally be in possession of a car like the Lotus and not be able to take flight. But Beau didn't know how she was traveling, and she wanted to keep it that way.

Information was just one of the things his money bought him, and she couldn't afford a ticket on her record.

Lola left California behind and crossed the border to Nevada, the only other state she'd been. She stopped at a motel in Salt Lake City in the late evening. There were few other people around. Just like she had in San Francisco, she paid the clerk in cash, bolted the door and shoved as much cash as would fit into the safe. With a bag of Doritos and a Coke from the vending machine, Lola sat on the bed and turned on the TV. She scarfed chips and flipped through every channel twice before shutting it off. The digital clock read 9:58 P.M.

On a whim, she changed into a bathing suit, took a threadbare towel and went to the pool. Having closed at ten, it was quiet and dark, so she hopped the short fence and got in the hot tub.

The door to her room was within her view. Always in the back of her mind was the cash. In the safe. In the car. Under the mattress. Stuffed into her jean pockets.

The night was cool, but the water was warm. She didn't turn on the bubbles, afraid they'd draw attention. For the second day in a row, she'd only spoken to motel clerks and gas station attendants. Even with them, she was cautious.

She set her head back against the edge, letting the heat soothe the stiffness in her neck. The drive from San Francisco had been long, but the road ahead of her was open, proof she was free. If she decided to go south instead of north, west instead of east, right instead of left—it didn't matter as long as she kept moving. She'd never believed in fate or destiny. There was always a master. Every choice, every decision she made put her on a new path. She wouldn't give anyone else power over her again.

Lola couldn't shake the feeling of a chain around her ankle, though. As if Beau would only let her get as far as he wanted, and when he decided he was ready, he'd start reeling her back in. She couldn't lose focus. The more distance she put between them, the stronger she became—but the opposite was also true.

She wiped beads of sweat from her hairline. She'd been away from him forty-eight hours, and he was hundreds of miles away. Was it far enough to save her from him? From herself? She sank deeper into the warm water—into the torture of another memory she knew she should forget.

Lola removed her new diamond earrings and set them on the bathroom counter. She glanced up at her reflection. Beau was in the doorway, his bowtie hanging around his neck, a shadow of stubble on his jaw. He came up behind her and slid his arms around her waist. "When did you change?" he whispered. "I wanted to watch."

"I never let you watch."

"That doesn't mean I don't."

Lola's heart skipped as he nuzzled her neck. The idea that he'd seen her undress without her permission made her flush. He was a dog—she knew that. He'd treated her like a dog. What made him think he could get away with that—standing just out of sight as she unzipped the long zippers of the dresses he'd bought her, unclipped the stockings of her wasted lingerie, unclasped her

31

heavy, expensive necklaces. "You watched me?" *she asked, her breath coming faster.*

"Mmm." He moved her hair aside and kissed a spot under her ear. "No. But it's been very tempting."

Lola inhaled a slinky breath and opened her eyes. She was hot everywhere, her body's memory of Beau much more favorable than her mind's. She got out of the spa, curled her toes over the edge of the dark pool and dove in. A November night in Salt Lake City wasn't the optimal time for a swim, but the biting water shocked her system. It jarred her in a necessary way, that sudden switch from hot to cold.

Chapter Five

Beau waited at the host's stand as a young girl wound through the diner's empty tables. She grabbed a laminated menu from its slot and popped her gum. "One?"

"Is Dina Winters working?" Beau asked.

"Yep."

"Seat me in her section."

"We don't have sections tonight," she said. "Just one waitress on duty."

Beau sat in a plastic booth and took the menu. Lola's love for breakfast food made sense if this was what her mom had fed her regularly. Everything at The Lucky Egg seemed to have eggs as an ingredient.

"I know you?" came a voice.

Beau looked up at a woman with burgundy hair and gray roots. Her apron folded between the rolls of her stomach. "Are you Dina?"

"Depends who's asking."

"I'm a friend of Lola's."

"Oh." She tapped the end of her pen against her order pad. "Then, yeah. That's my daughter."

"Do you have a minute?"

She looked around the restaurant. "I got lots of minutes, but what's this about? Is Lola all right?"

Beau gestured to the seat across from him. "I just want to talk. I'll pay for your time." It came out like a bad habit. Money solved his problems all the time, but he wondered when it'd become second nature—especially outside of work.

Dina snorted but didn't object. The booth whooshed when she sat. "You got ten seconds to tell me what you're after."

"Lola."

"Nine seconds."

"Have you seen her?"

"Since when?"

He rubbed his chin. "Forty-eight hours?"

The woman laughed. "You got the wrong person. I think I've talked to her two or three times in as many years. Johnny calls now and then, good boy that he is. If not for him, I wouldn't know nothing about her."

Beau looked at the table. He'd doubted she'd know much, but this was worse. His palms began to sweat.

"She owe you money or something?"

"No," Beau said emphatically, looking up again. "I'm just trying to get in touch with her."

"Oh. Well, she works at a bar not too far from here on Sunset Strip. Hey Joe—you know it?"

34

Beau scrubbed his palm over his stubbled jawline and nodded. "I know the place."

"She's got a boyfriend, though—Johnny. And he's good to her. So whatever you're after, might be best you just walk away."

"Thanks for the tip," he said dryly.

"Sure. Now, what can I get you?"

Beau cocked his head. "What?"

She pointed her pen at the menu. "To eat, honey."

"I don't care." He slid it away. "Whatever you recommend. Breakfast food."

"Coming right up."

He considered leaving. If Dina thought Lola was still with Johnny, she was worse off than him. She waddled over to the counter, ripped off his ticket and refilled a water glass at the only other table with a customer. Beau didn't want breakfast food. He wanted to find Lola.

His cell vibrated in his pocket, and he answered it immediately. "Bragg?"

"More dead ends. I can't find anyone named Lola Winters staying in the area. I can go national, but can you give me some kind of direction? Maybe a favorite spot?"

Beau had nothing. He could probably rule out Las Vegas since she'd been there. Apparently, that was how well he knew the woman he'd fallen in love with. "Motels?" Beau asked.

"Nope."

"Airports? Car rentals? Fucking train stations?"

Bragg was silent.

"Damn it," Beau said.

"There's one thing I haven't tried. Hospital and jail records."

Beau looked down at the table. For a shameful moment, he preferred that to the alternative. In jail, in a hospital, she would need him. There'd be no pretense. He could handle those situations better than anyone he knew, whether it was getting her the best care or paying off whomever he needed to if she were in trouble. Anything was better than not knowing why. Or where. Or if. If she'd really left on purpose, or if this was all some big misunderstanding.

"Search them," Beau said. "Every few hours until we know more."

He hung up as Dina set an oversized dish of French toast in front of him. It must've been a joke. Lola had to be watching from the kitchen, laughing at him in her carefree way. Like the time she'd thrown her body into his arms and wrapped her legs around his waist.

"...come have breakfast in bed with me," she said.

"If you insist, though I don't really see the point."

"There's no point. This isn't a negotiation or a board meeting where there needs to be an explanation for everything. There's absolutely no fucking point at all, and that is the point."

Beau understood that conversation better now, after having spent more time with her. He was the one who'd set parameters around his life, and he was the one who could tear them down. Breakfast for dinner. Eating where he slept. They were childish things, but they weren't illegal—he'd gawked at her as if they were.

"Come on. Eat up," Dina said. "It was Lola's favorite. Mine too."

Beau took a reluctant, painful, memory-filled bite. His mouthful of syrup tasted like Lola.

"Can I get you anything else?" Dina asked.

Beau needed her to keep talking so he could survive that French toast. For the first time in two days, he didn't feel an ounce of anger. "Did she grow up near here?"

Dina glanced around the diner. Her other customer had his eyes glued to the overhead TV set. "Five or so minutes away," she said. "How'd you say you know her?"

Beau wiped his mouth with a napkin and cleared his throat. "I guess you could say we worked together once."

"Oh." Her mom nodded high, keeping her eyes on Beau. "I see. Well, Lola only worked at two places in her life, so I got a pretty good idea what you're getting at."

Beau didn't look away, though he wanted to. When had he ever faced the family of someone he'd screwed over? Beyond Johnny, he'd never considered how hurting Lola might extend to those who loved her.

"Hang on," Dina said. "There was that 7-Eleven she worked at for a while as a cover up for what she was really doing. She must've thought I was dumb to believe money like that came from selling bubblegum and cigarettes." Her smile fell. "Completely slipped my mind. But no, I'm not about to believe that's where you know her from."

Beau smiled thinly. "It's not." Walking into a 7-Eleven years ago and coming face to face with a young Lola might've changed his life. Before his money, he'd been like any other boy trying to get a girl's attention. For the most part, he was too distracted by work to care, but he couldn't imagine walking away from Lola back then, before he'd ever tasted power—or rejection.

"She never worked here?" he asked.

"This place? You mean the diner with quicksand floors?" She laughed at her joke. "People get stuck here. Mario in the kitchen came in to use the restroom twenty years ago. I didn't want that for her. She can do better than her old lady."

"Lola's very smart," Beau agreed.

"Pity she got stuck on the Strip," she said.

"At Cat Shoppe, you mean?"

Dina eyed him. "No. I'm talking about Hey Joe, where I said she works now. Not that I did any better for myself, but I wanted her to become something. She was a proud little girl, though."

"Pride's not always a bad thing."

"You don't watch out, pride'll get you. Lola didn't want nobody telling her what to do, especially me. Thought she knew better. She had a fighting spirit. Too much. Then she hooked up with Johnny, and he calmed her down lots, but while she's with him, she won't go much of anywhere." Dina was barely looking at him anymore. "Johnny's a good man, but sometimes I wonder where she'd be now if she hadn't met him. Maybe this whole side of town's quicksand."

A hint of thickness in her voice made Beau wonder if she missed her daughter. "Why don't you two speak?"

Dina shook her head slowly and looked up at the ceiling a moment. "I wasn't a good mom. I know that. She knew it too since she was little. Like you said—she's smart. Smarter than anyone in my family."

Beau'd heard enough of Lola's childhood to know Dina could've done better. The fact that she kept Lola out of the diner said something, though. She saw the same potential in Lola Beau had. "I'm sure you weren't as bad as you think."

She snorted. "When I got pregnant with her, I quit smoking. Not because I was worried about the baby, but because it made me sick. Nausea, heartburn, all that. I was pissed about it, thought it was unfair. I loved my cigarettes. What's that say about me?"

One of her bushy eyebrows crinkled. He wanted to tell her that everybody made mistakes and that most people never copped to them. They went on thinking they'd been good people. Beau had seen it in business time and time again—those who owned their mistakes, like Beau, were successful because they didn't make them a second time.

"Anyway, when I found out about the stripping," she continued, "I told her to stop. Said I hadn't done much for her in my life, but I was putting my foot down. I think that made her want to do it more."

So Lola had been stubborn from the start. It didn't surprise him, and he understood why someone like Johnny had tried to tame her. Wild horses were as easy to lose as they were to love. "Were you ever close?"

"No. I never planned for her. It was her dad who wanted a kid until he had one. He bolted when he realized it wasn't all fun and games. Took me a lifetime to get over it, but that doesn't mean I didn't want good things for her."

It'd been a while since Beau had taken an interest in anyone's life when it didn't benefit him. Even Brigitte. He set down his fork and got comfortable in his seat. "Tell me more."

"Not much to tell. She was young when he left, and I got all the responsibility I never wanted. And no money, either. He took what little we had, the low-life scum. Anyway, I'm not trying to dump the past on you—not like I even think about this anymore. You asked why we don't speak—answer's that we just don't got anything to say to each other. She lets Johnny do the talking."

"Sounds like the same bull-headed Lola I know." Syrup dripped over the sides of his toast, pooling on Beau's plate. "Knew, I mean."

"You work downtown?"

Beau looked up again. Dina's eyes were narrowed on him. "Am I that obvious?" he muttered.

"You don't look like you belong in these parts."

"These parts? This is Hollywood, for God's sake. It's not like we're on Skid Row."

"You just don't look like it."

"I grew up not far from here," Beau said defensively. He was beginning to think it was more than just his suit that gave him away. It shouldn't have bothered him that he'd risen so high above his social beginnings, he was unrecognizable to his peers—he'd worked hard for that kind of esteem—but it did. He'd been one of them once. And his success hadn't come without struggle or sacrifice. "For twenty-seven years, I barely had enough to get by. I didn't grow up spoiled or privileged. Why is that so hard for everyone to believe?"

Dina's face was harder now. "Tell me what you're really doing here."

"I already did. Looking for a girl I used to know who told me once her mother worked at The Lucky Egg."

"Sounds suspicious as get out to me. Not sure what you're after, but if it's good for Melody, I hope you find it. If it's not, you'll have Johnny to answer to."

"What did you just say?" Beau asked.

"You heard me, young man. You're not exactly someone I'd want to mess with, but neither's Johnny, and he—"

"No, not that. Melody?" The name was vaguely familiar, something he'd heard recently.

"Oh. Lola's a nickname her daddy gave her, but I call her by her given name when I get worked up. Doctor doesn't like me to get worked up. I got high cholesterol, which you can probably guess—"

Beau stood, digging his wallet out of his jacket pocket. He remembered where he'd heard that name. He'd thought it was a stage name, and Lola had been teasing him in the strip club when she'd insisted he call her that. Maybe it'd been a clue—right in front of him the whole time.

"Hey, you barely touched your breakfast," Dina said. "Don't you like French toast?"

"I like it fine." Beau set a hundred-dollar bill on the table.

"Honey, I don't got change for that."

"Said I'd pay you for your time." Beau was nearly one foot out the door. He stopped himself from saying she'd earned it. Maybe it wasn't his suit that gave him away, but comments like that. "Thanks for your help," he said instead.

Chapter Six

In the past week, Lola had seen more of the world than she had in all twenty-nine years of her life. It was exhilarating, liberating, exciting. She covered her mouth for a yawn. Well, not all of it. Beau had been right about at least one thing—the world's largest ball of twine underwhelmed.

Lola stared at the popular roadside attraction, trying to warm her hands in the pockets of her denim jacket. She'd only been there five minutes, and she was ready to leave, but she'd driven through far stretches of countryside to get there. It really was just a big, stinky ball, though.

Lola giggled as Beau's comment came back to her.

"Big balls don't do anything for me. But if they impress you, I can show you a couple—"

A grown man was now hugging the ball as a woman photographed him. Lola looked around to see if anyone else was having the same immature reaction she was, the one Beau would've had too if he were there.

Beau took himself too seriously, but he had his moments. In a way, because his silly side was infrequent, it made him more endearing. She couldn't envision him letting his guard down that way with many other people.

Lola sighed and took a picture of the twine ball with a digital camera she'd purchased. If she'd had someone to text it to, she would've sent it along with some witty comment. Of course, she would've needed a phone for that.

"Want me to take one with you in it?" asked the woman with the ball-hugging man.

"No, thank you."

"You sure? Take it from me—when you get home, the pictures with no one in them get old real fast."

Lola suppressed a smile. Everyone else was doing it, but she couldn't help feeling a little ridiculous. "Okay," she said. "Why not."

"Anyone you want in it?"

Lola shook her head. "I'm alone." She handed the woman her camera. When it was her turn, she stood just in front of the ball and smiled. She refused to hug it.

"Good one." The woman returned Lola's camera. "You'll be glad when you get back. That's definitely going in the scrapbook."

Lola thanked her and left. During her trip, whenever she'd remembered, she'd taken at least one photo at each stop. At a rodeo in Wyoming, she'd sat in the stands with her cotton candy and watched a roping competition. Afterward, she'd won a goldfish at the state fair and given it to a little girl, making her hold it up for the camera. Lola had never been much of a moviegoer, but in Denver, she'd spent two days in the dark, gorging on foreign films during a festival. She'd photographed the sun rising between two gray mountains. A group of oddly-shaped pine cones. Tree trunks floating in the fog. Those were all from an early-morning hike she'd taken. She wasn't in any of the pictures, though, and she wasn't sure why she had them. They weren't for a scrapbook—or for anything, really.

Lola stretched her arms and legs before getting back behind the wheel. Driving an entire country could be hard on the body, and she was achy a lot of the time. She unfolded her map panel by panel, revealing America in seconds. Without a phone or GPS, navigation was a new skill for her. The options were many—Botanical Gardens in Des Moines, the St. Louis Arch, Chicago—but she'd already decided on the Ozark Mountains. After days of cities and crowds, solitude in nature sounded luxurious.

Lola put the car in drive and hit the freeway. Hours crept by, as endless as the yellow, rolling wheat all around her. Clouds skidded across the blue sky and as she drove into the afternoon, they began to gather, low and gray on the horizon.

Everything had darkened by the time she reached the Ozarks, even though it was only late afternoon. She scanned her way through radio static, searching for a weather report. Thunder rumbled in the distance. The map got fuzzy around the mountains, and she didn't want to get caught in the rain looking for lodging.

She pulled off the road at the first place she saw,

her tires chomping as she found a place to park. In her Hey Joe hoodie and a jacket, the warmest things she'd brought from California besides her trench coat, she walked up to a tiny, hole-in-the-wall bar with a lit Fat Tire sign in the window.

Inside, Lola blinked a few times to adjust her eyes to the dark. It was empty—nobody drinking his dinner yet. The interior wasn't an exact replica of Hey Joe, but they were cut from the same cigarette-burned cloth. She walked up to the bar. Johnny's third favorite Led Zeppelin song, "Babe I'm Gonna Leave You," played in the background as if someone'd forgotten to turn the music back up after a conversation. Some postcards of Midwest attractions were tacked on the walls. The retouched photographs were more vivid than what Lola'd seen with her own eyes. The real thing had been good, but it could always be better.

Lola hadn't contacted anyone, though she'd often thought about it. A message that she was fine. Better than fine. Amazing. She was seeing things that were good enough for postcards, learning about the country she'd grown up in—and herself too.

Above a wall of hard alcohol was a photo of bikini-clad women in snow boots and furry hats.

It may be freezing outside, but Missouri is still the hottest state in the U.S.A.!

She smiled. In Denver, she'd almost bought that same postcard with *Colorado* instead of *Missouri*. It would've made Beau laugh. She looked forward to a time when her tinges of nostalgia would die off, and she could fully enjoy Beau's suffering.

The bar served food, only three items—hamburger, hotdog or cheese fries. And then a list of beer sorted by draft or bottle. Lola hadn't eaten since Kansas. Sometimes, during long stretches in the car, she'd wonder what would've happened if she'd walked into that gas station weeks earlier and Beau hadn't had a gun to his head. If they'd bought a couple pieces of candy and scarfed hotdogs on the way back to the hotel.

She slid a hand along the pitted lip of the bar. The wood wasn't as smooth as Hey Joe's. Or maybe that was just how she remembered it. It wouldn't have mattered—the hotdogs. Beau would've gotten what he'd wanted from her one way or another. If not that night, then the next. Or the next. Beau never gave up. Did he?

Lola hadn't seen the look on Beau's face when she'd disappeared. With his control issues, it would be the not knowing that'd quickly drive him insane—where had she gone? How? Would she be back? When? Those questions, over and over, until he didn't know what was stronger—the hurt or the anger. Until he was teetering between never wanting to see her again and questioning how he could go on without her.

Lola turned to leave the bar but stopped. A tall, burly man dressed in black blocked the doorway. He stomped his leather boots on the ground, shaking out his long, brown-and-gray-streaked hair. "Help you?" he asked.

She checked over her shoulder, absentmindedly

patting her wallet in her pocket. The alarming amount of cash she had in her car and on her person was never far from her mind. Nor were strange, oversized men who might be on the lookout for women traveling alone. "No. I was just on my way into town."

"Better get a move on then."

She edged around him, glancing sidelong at the patches on his motorcycle cut before deciding to keep her eyes on his face. This guy looked meaner than the diluted versions of him she'd served in Hollywood. He shifted to let her by.

With her first step outside, something dripped on the crown of her head. The sky slumped, resting on the mountains. A white spec floated down and landed on her face. "What the...?"

"First snow of the season."

She glanced back at the man, who leaned in the doorway. "*Snow?*"

"Yep."

She'd only seen machine-made snow once—on the ground in Big Bear. This was something else completely. More flakes drifted down on her, glitter in a snow globe, dampening the top of her hair. She put her tongue out to catch some. It was natural that something other than rain fell from the sapphire-gray sky, but it was foreign to her—like reading about music and then hearing it for the first time.

"It's beautiful." Lola blinked crystals off her lashes. "I've never seen anything like it. It's—"

"Goddamn obnoxious. You ever shoveled this shit? Plus, it brings on the insomnia, the cold." He paused. "But you know how that is."

She squinted at him over her shoulder. "No. I sleep fine."

"Dark circles don't lie." He disappeared back into the bar.

She touched her cheek—she'd noticed them too. All that driving left her restless at night.

The parking lot was empty. Her car glowed red against the muted gravel, the buzz in the air tainted by the smell of petroleum. For eight days, she'd convinced herself staying under the radar was necessary. She'd barely spoken to anyone. She wanted to tell someone how amazing it was that she'd never seen this before. Lola pulled her jacket closer around her and shivered.

The magic of the moment was short-lived for the same reason her one-handed picture while crossing the Golden Gate Bridge had come out blurry. She was alone. Beau could've been standing by her side for her first snowfall if he hadn't been so proud and childish. He was a grown man behaving like a boy who'd had his feelings hurt. Was that what he thought of Lola, that she'd taken her toys and disappeared in the middle of the night?

They hurt themselves to hurt each other. It was almost as if Lola could look past the pain when she saw it that way—she just wasn't sure she was ready to.

Chapter Seven

Lola stood in front of the roadside bar in the Ozarks, snow falling a little faster now, dampening her denim jacket and hoodie.

"Not much of a coat you got there."

Lola turned quickly at the gruff voice. The man in the leather boots was back. "I'm from California," she said.

He held out a paper cup. "Here."

She shuffled toward him a little, the soles of her sneakers scraping against the dusty-brush sidewalk. The drink instantly warmed her hand.

"So, you lost, California?" he asked.

She inhaled fresh coffee and took a sip. "No."

"Liar."

She almost spit out her drink, raising her eyebrows at him. "What?"

He nodded at her pocket, where she'd stuffed the guidebook. She'd folded the corner of a page that had information about a nearby lodge.

"What brings you around?" he asked. "Business? Pleasure?"

She took another drink, too quickly this time, and burnt her tongue. She ran the tip of it over the roof of her mouth, her eyes watering. He didn't strike her as anything other than curious, but she'd thought the same of Beau when she'd met him. "Mostly sightseeing."

"Anything good so far?"

"Sure." She angled her body a little more in his direction. "I stood in the geographic center of the continental United States."

He laughed. "Well, that's something, isn't it?"

Lola nodded. It'd been more exciting than the twine, at least.

"Where you headed?" he asked.

She glanced upward. Information was precious. "I…"

"Give me that." He held out his hand for the guidebook, so she passed it to him. He flipped to the dog-eared page and grumbled, "Moose Lodge. It's for tourists, you know."

She shrugged. "Aren't all hotels?"

"Got a point. Not much to see around here, though."

Lola frowned. She didn't mind that. The open road and countryside had been good for her. The snow was magical. Kind of like Los Angeles from a distance when it was all lit up at night. Her heart thumped once when she thought of home.

"This lodge isn't far," he said. "You by yourself?"

Lola glanced at the lid of her coffee. She palmed the cup, welcoming its warmth. Yes, she was by herself. No, Beau was not waiting in the car for her. He was where she'd left him, where she'd spent twenty-nine years of her life—minus eight days.

"Ah," the man said. "I see what you got now, and it ain't insomnia."

"What is it?" Lola asked, still looking down.

"Lonely. I got that too, plus the insomnia, ever since my wife passed. Not a nice combo."

Lola nodded, swallowing. Things were rarely as bad as they seemed when she looked outside herself. "How long were you married?"

"Almost twenty years."

"Long time," Lola murmured. A long time to screw things up, to break each other's hearts. A long time to put them back together.

"She had cancer," he continued. "But you know how she died? Hit by a car. Believe that?"

"I'm sorry," Lola said lamely.

"So was I, until I realized all the ways Maxie makes me better, even from the grave. Just this morning, I drive a few towns over to Costco and someone's pulling out of a front spot. Never happens, right? I wait a good couple minutes. Then this guy comes from the other direction, swipes it at the last second. You know what I did?"

Lola hesitated, almost afraid to ask. "What?"

"Before Maxie passed, I would've taught the scrawny shit some manners. Instead, I rolled down the window and said, 'You know what? Take the goddamn spot. I'll park in back, get myself some exercise.'"

Lola chewed her bottom lip, trying to connect that back to their conversation. She'd never been much of a religious person, so she wasn't sure of the polite way to proceed. "So, you're saying...that was Maxie's way of keeping you fit?"

He chuckled, shaking his head. "I'm saying since she left me, I don't sweat the small stuff. Actually, I don't let the big stuff get to me anymore either. Because it's really not that important if you think about it. I'm going to go to Costco lots more times before I die, God willing, but never again with her. I'd park in the back every day if it meant she were walking by my side."

Lola's nose tingled. What Beau had done wasn't small stuff by any means. Not to her. It wasn't like he'd stolen her parking spot. This man would agree if he heard her story. Wouldn't he? He'd lost the love of his life—well, so had she, and it wasn't either of their faults. To forgive Beau would be a betrayal to herself—she'd always believed that. But maybe this man was telling her the opposite was true. Forgiveness was the path back to herself, to the woman who'd never gone out of her way to hurt someone else the way she had Beau.

"Life is short," Lola said in summary.

"That's right. We'd better try to have a good time while we're here." He rubbed his hands together, warming them. "So, what're you running from, California?"

"What makes you think I'm running at all?"

He raised his brows at her. "My family's owned this bar since before I could walk. Seen a lot of people pass through this town because it's quiet. Hidden. Sometimes women trying to escape with their lives."

"It's not like that." Lola shook her head. Running away was weak. She was taking back her life, fortifying herself after years of living for others. "I'm starting over."

"That's what a lot of these women say. Sometimes they get caught. Most of the time they go back on their own. But they're almost always hiding." The man raised his coffee cup at her. "Somebody were going after my wife, I'd want to know about it."

Lola slid her wallet out of her back pocket. Suddenly, she wanted to be alone the way she had been her whole trip. It felt as if she were on the verge of understanding what all this had been about. She didn't want to lose that. "How much do I owe you for the coffee?"

"On the house. As for Moose Lodge, you're going to take this road down another mile and turn right. It'll be on your left." He returned her guidebook. "Get home safe, wherever home is."

Lola didn't have a home anymore. Johnny had come close, but that feeling of safety had vanished quicker than she thought possible. Now, only one idea came to mind—but an empty shell was no place for anyone to call home.

◆ ◆ ◆

Lola found the lodge easily, and it was a good thing, because the storm was picking up. Her Converse crunched snow as she walked up to the lobby. Inside, she removed her hood, plucking her sweater to rid it of flakes.

"Early this year, isn't it?"

Lola looked up at a young girl, whose eager smile gave her chipmunk cheeks. "What?"

She nodded behind Lola. "The snow. I thought we'd have a few more weeks."

"Oh. I wouldn't know. This is my first time in Missouri." She approached the front desk. "First snowfall too."

The girl clapped her hands and wiggled her pink-tipped fingers. "How exciting. I don't even remember my first. I was a baby."

Lola laughed a little at that. Enthusiasm was infectious in this friendly town. "I would've called ahead if I'd realized there was a storm coming. Do you have a room for tonight?"

"We sure do." She grabbed the computer mouse and began clicking. "King bed all right? All the rooms are one-fifty plus tax."

It was the most Lola'd paid for a room yet, but she wasn't about to go hunting for something else in this weather. It wasn't like she didn't have the money. "I'll take it."

"Great. Just give me a sec while I set you up."

A wailing noise came from outside. Lola left a couple hundred-dollar bills on the counter with her license and went to the window, drawing the curtain aside.

It was dusk now, but the pine trees surrounding the Moose Lodge glowed white with powdered branches. A little boy in a puffy jacket and knit cap cried noisily, gulping air. His mom stood by their car, hunched over her phone to protect it from the snow. Lola had the urge to go pick him up, comfort him, anything to stop his bawling.

After a minute, the mom snatched a toy airplane from her purse and handed it to him. His face smoothed immediately, and he took off running, his arms planed at his sides as he weaved through the tree trunks. She'd done the same with her doll, Nadia, as a little girl. She'd dressed it up for imaginary tea parties. At home alone, that was her friend, and that was enough to content her. Children played games for themselves, not their opponents.

Lola crinkled her nose with an unexpected wave of tears. Either she was hormonal or homesick, because thinking of her past wasn't the kind of thing that usually moved her.

The boy jumped into fresh snow with both feet. If Lola'd brought proper boots, she would've joined him. She decided when she had a kid, she'd make sure he or she got a chance to play in the snow. And she'd be right by his side.

His mother stayed in the parking lot, tapping at her cellphone. Lola's cash-filled car was ten feet away.

Johnny'd had a mantra—no kids until they had the money. Well, Lola was sitting on hundreds of thousands of dollars now. That kind of money was a new home, a college fund, clean clothes and never missing a meal. Lola had put all that and more on the line just to spite Beau. She'd not only lost touch with the future she'd once wanted, but every day that money wasn't in a bank, she'd also risked it. For what? To hide out in motels in hopes of making Beau suffer? Who was actually suffering?

Lola'd been avoiding thinking of where and when her trip would end, but she had to start making decisions. She'd hoped to get some answers from the road, and in that moment, one came to her—Los Angeles was her home. Before Beau, before Johnny, it'd been her first true love, and it was where she one day wanted to watch her own son or daughter run around in her backyard.

She'd been looking for the wrong thing. True freedom would never come with revenge. Lola had spent a decade angry with her mother for reasons she couldn't even pinpoint—she didn't need that shadow at her back looming larger. She wanted herself and those she loved to live in light.

"Oh, shoot," she heard from behind her. "We don't accept cash."

Lola turned back to the front desk. The lodge was a step up from the motels she'd been crashing at, but not a huge one. "You don't? My credit card is..." Lola hesitated as she returned to the counter. "Is there any way you can make an exception? I've been traveling for over a week and haven't had a problem paying cash anywhere else."

"My dad, he's strict about it." The girl shook her head. "We need to swipe a card at check-in and have it for incidentals and stuff. We had some problems before."

Lola took the money back and nodded. Finding another place at this time of night and in these snowy mountains wouldn't be easy, but it wasn't impossible. She could even go back to the big man at the small bar and ask for his help.

But Lola was beginning to question the fact that she'd taken so many chances already. She took out an emergency credit card hidden in her wallet and handed it over. The girl grinned again and swiped it.

Lola decided in the morning, she'd deposit her money in a bank. Driving around with as much cash as she had in her trunk had been reckless. One day, she'd have a family, and she had put them at risk. The price for revenge suddenly seemed much too high.

Chapter Eight

Melody. Lola. Had he even fucking known her? Beau entered all his interactions with at least a small amount of cynicism and distrust. It'd served him well in affairs both business and personal. But Lola represented a time before he'd had to be that man. When she'd kicked a car outside of Hey Joe, he'd been just as attracted to her as he had seeing her on stage at Cat Shoppe. He should've walked away based on the fact that he hadn't wanted to. Something in her blue eyes had kept him planted on that sidewalk, though. She'd inched closer and closer, peering at him in the dark, neon lights reflecting off her shiny black hair. Some predators stalked their prey. Others waited for their prey to come to them. In those few seconds as she'd approached him, he hadn't been sure which one of them was predator and which was prey. Even before his money, he'd never had that feeling before. But he'd recovered quickly. He was Beau Olivier—and he was nobody's dinner.

"Olivier."

Beau looked up from the presentation binder in front of him. His business partner stood at the head of the conference table. Lawrence Thorne was the other half of Bolt Ventures, and one of the only people Beau trusted. But that was all their relationship'd ever been. Larry had a wife Beau knew from myriad events and two kids Beau'd only met once.

"Think you might want to wake the fuck up?" Lawrence asked. "It's four in the afternoon."

Their lawyer, Louis, rapped his pen on the table. "You've been silent the entire meeting. Since when do you have no comment on the fact that VenTech's stock closed at a record low?"

Beau furrowed his eyebrows and turned the page to a graph labeled *Potential Holdings Research Report— VenTech*. The squiggly line had dipped far into the red. That always caught his attention, but he hadn't noticed it in the twenty minutes they'd been sitting there. Instead, he'd been thinking about the former holding who'd taken a nosedive into disastrous territory.

"This was today?" Beau asked.

Louis nodded. "Word is, they're done for."

Beau looked at both of them. "Then let's move."

"We have people looking into it," Larry said.

"I'm tired of waiting." Beau'd been patient as always, and as always, it'd paid off. But he had his limits, and he was ready to pounce on VenTech, the company that'd bought his payment services website ten years ago and picked it apart until it was nothing more than a carcass. Now, Beau was in a position to save VenTech from bankruptcy. He wanted to look the founder, George Wright, in the eye, and tell him he owned him. He leaned forward on his elbows. "Draw up the offer."

"You're sure?" Larry asked. "Established companies aren't really our thing."

"VenTech is desperate. You know I've been tracking them for a long time. You promised me the day we partnered, Larry—you'd back me up on this."

Larry nodded. "I did. And if this is what you need, I'm on board."

"Good. Get the paperwork started."

"Consider it done." Louis reclined back in his seat, steepling his fingers. "So, you going to tell us whose call you're expecting?"

Beau slid the binder away. "I don't know what you're talking about."

"Last time you were like this," Louis said, "you were wooing a new company but wouldn't tell us which one. You've been checking your phone like an addict waiting to hear about a fix. So who is it?"

Beau glanced in the direction of his office. If he moved now, he could have a drink in his hand in under sixty seconds. "It's personal."

Larry snorted. "Bullshit. What's more important to you than this?"

"I don't know," Beau said, "maybe an ear infection?"

"You're mad because I left in the middle of the day last week to take my kid to the ER?" Larry asked. "The fuck's wrong with you, man?"

"I'm not mad." Beau ran his hands through his hair. "I'm saying maybe I've got my own shit to deal with too, yet I'm here more than anyone else."

"So take an afternoon off. You're the one who wants to be here all the time."

Louis nodded. "You don't need anyone to tell you when you can go home for the day. You got plenty of underlings around here who live to pick up the slack."

None of this was news to Beau. Larry had started going home at five a couple years ago, and the office had survived. Thrived, even, without one more opinion in the mix.

"I'll be honest, Beau." Larry shut his laptop and sat. "You look like shit. Even more than when we're going through a rough acquisition. I think productivity might pick up if you take your gloomy ass out to a matinee or something. Treat yourself to a haircut while you're at it."

"Fuck you, Thorne," Beau said, but his heart wasn't in it.

Larry just smiled.

Beau reached in his jacket for his phone but stopped when Larry and Louis exchanged a glance. He didn't need to check it anyway. He tested his ringer several times a day, and it was working fine. He'd ignored two calls from Brigitte that morning just out of sheer anger that it hadn't been Detective Bragg calling.

It'd been eight goddamn days since Lola had left. If this was a game for Lola, she hadn't left him a single clue. The leather pants and T-shirt she'd worn the night he'd met her were gone, but other than that, he didn't know what else she'd taken with her. Nothing he'd bought her, except what she'd been wearing that night. Bragg was also frustrated. He'd had better luck tracking down criminals with actual reasons to hide. Criminals who preyed on young, beautiful women traveling alone with lots of cash.

Beau was always hot lately, but with that thought, warmth traveled to his feet and scalp. Waking up with Lola, coming home to her—it'd been a new, irregular world, but she'd centered him. Now, a week later, he didn't even know if she was dead or alive. That seemed unfair. If anyone should get to decide her fate, it should be him. He at least wanted that choice again.

More and more, he worried she hadn't been real, just a dream. They shared none of the same friends or daily routines. There wasn't anywhere on his way to work where he'd stop and remember a moment they'd had. Had she been an illusion, a sleek magic trick? His last moments with her, he'd been dumb with lust, two fingers inside her sweet pussy silk.

Beau laced his hands in his hair, suddenly aware of how long it was, and that he'd forgotten to style it that morning. He stood. "I need some fresh air."

"Yeah, fine, just don't come back today," Larry said dismissively. "Go home or something."

Beau didn't go home, and he didn't get air. He went to his office and looked out his window with a drink in his hand.

Orange skyscrapers reflected the late afternoon. Where was she, his beautiful kitten, that sly minx? All by herself, no trail left behind? Was she wearing her skintight leather pants and asking for trouble? Was she flirting with men who could hurt her far worse than Beau had?

Beau unbuttoned his collar. He couldn't get his breathing under control. Work was supposed to be where he found balance. He would've slammed his fist into the window except that he'd hit a few things over the last few days, and it never seemed to do any good. The leather pants bothered him. He couldn't stop picturing her in them.

He'd lost track of how many times he'd listed in his head all the things he knew about Lola. The food she ate. The drinks she drank. Any mentions she'd made of places she'd wanted to see or things she'd wanted to buy. He didn't think it'd be as easy as showing up at the world's largest ball of twine and finding her there, but he'd called the box office anyway. They didn't attach names to cash transactions, and why would they?

Lola had more money now than she must've ever dreamed. When Beau had sold his company, he'd signed on the dotted line and gone from thousands in debt to a multi-millionaire. Sex had been suddenly and oppressively on his mind. He'd wanted to fuck with all the power he'd finally had. Lola had taken that away from him—that little cat, with big blue eyes and black, furry triangle ears, had captivated him from the moment he'd walked into Cat Shoppe. It was as if she'd called his eyes right to her. He'd just been handed the key to his kingdom, and he could've had anything he'd wanted— and what he'd wanted stood underneath a white spotlight, dressed in nothing but a diamond bikini and cat ears. She became the one thing he needed that night and the one thing he couldn't have. With four words— *"I'm not for sale"*—he wasn't enough again, not even as a man with something to offer.

Lola would know that same power now—because of him. Because of him, she was out there in her leather pants—fucking, drinking, spending cash, laughing at him. Beau'd thought he was the one in charge, but just the sway of her hips had disarmed him long enough to steal his power a second time. He was halfway between wanting to worship her and wring her neck for pulling this off. His heart pounded at the thought of holding that slender column under his fingers as she begged his forgiveness.

His phone beeped, and he jumped. His hands were curled into two tight fists.

"Mr. Olivier?" came his assistant's voice.

"What?" he snapped. "What the fuck is it?"

It was a moment before she continued. "I-I'm sorry. You said—you were very clear that I should interrupt you any time Detective Bragg called."

Beau turned from the window. He leaned his knuckles on his desk and spoke directly into the phone, as if that would get him answers faster. "He called?"

"Just now."

"Why didn't he try my cell?"

"He said he did."

Beau took out his phone to see he had a missed call. "Piece of shit," he muttered, tossing it aside. "Get Bragg for me. Now."

"He's already on the line," she said. "And he says he's got something for you."

Chapter Nine

Beau came home to a light on in the kitchen. His heart in his throat, he hung his coat on the hook by the door. Nobody'd been home to greet him since Lola'd left eight days ago. The housekeeper had been there that day, but she didn't leave lights on. Beau'd explained to her how that was a waste of money. And she didn't cook him dinner. He followed the smell of food and the clinking of dishware.

The weight that already sat on his shoulders grew heavier with each step. A few nights before Lola had left, she'd made pulled pork tacos in a "Kiss the Cook" apron she'd bought herself. She'd kept his food at the perfect temperature until he'd walked through the door, and it was the sexiest thing he'd ever seen—Lola, in a red-and-white gingham apron, making him dinner with barbeque sauce on her cheek. He'd kissed her, cleaning her face with a restrained lick of his tongue.

Beau held as breath as he entered the kitchen. Despite his conversation with Bragg an hour earlier, he half expected to find the same thing in the kitchen he had two weeks ago.

And that was exactly what he found—except that it was Brigitte wearing the apron, and she had something in the oven instead of the slow cooker.

Her face lit up as she raised a glass of red wine. "Welcome home. I thought you could use a homemade meal."

Beau clamped his mouth shut as his stomach turned, his eyes glued to that kitschy fucking apron and the barbeque sauce stain near the hem. "Where'd you find that?"

"What?" Brigitte followed his gaze down. "The apron? Hanging in the pantry. Honestly, I was surprised you even owned—"

"It was Lola's." Sweat formed on his hairline. Of course he wasn't going to find Lola in his kitchen. If she had any sense, she'd be terrified to ever face him again. He unknotted his tie and slid it off. "I told you to get rid of her shit."

Brigitte shrugged and grinned blue, her mouth tinted from the wine. "It's just an apron. Don't erupt, Mt. Olivier." She walked over and gave him her glass. "Drink this. It'll calm you."

Beau took the wine and set it on the counter. "I don't need to calm down. Your car isn't in the driveway."

"Warner brought me. He's the only person who ever checks on me." She blew out a heavy sigh, heaving

70

her chest and shoulders. "I hadn't seen a soul in two whole days, and I couldn't get you on the phone. What, did you smash it again? Anyway, I absolutely couldn't take another minute. I had to come over."

"You'll have to learn to deal with being alone, Brigitte. I don't want company right now."

She plumped her lower lip. "I'll try not to take that personally. What's the matter?"

Beau removed everything from his pockets into a dish on the counter. He didn't need Brigitte in his business, adding her two cents at every juncture. "Long day. That's all."

"You've been so distant since you kicked me out. You know I don't do well on my own, Beau."

He picked up the clean pile of mail his housekeeper had organized and sorted. "I've had a lot on my plate. And I didn't kick you out. There just wasn't enough room here for both you and her."

"Does that mean I can come back?"

Beau glanced up. Her eyebrows were raised. So that was why she was there—to scope things out and see if he might be distracted enough to let her back in. He didn't have the energy to argue, and it made no difference to him if she was there. His house had turned from sanctuary to hell now that he'd glimpsed a life he couldn't have. And Brigitte there, cooking for him, was a thorny reminder. "I don't care. Just take off that fucking apron."

Beau's phone rang. He checked the screen, saw it was Bragg, and cleared it. He'd call him as soon as he went upstairs to change. If he rushed off to his study,

Brigitte would pick at him until he spilled everything to her.

"Who was that?"

"Nobody." Beau opened a bill and tossed it aside, having already paid it online. He made a note to switch it over to e-mail and picked up another envelope, avoiding Brigitte's penetrating stare, her loud silence. Finally, he sighed and looked up. "What?"

"It's about her, isn't it?"

"Who?"

"Come on, Beau. You know who. There's something going on with Lola."

"I hardly think of her."

"You must think I'm blind. Tell me."

Beau slid his mail away and set his elbows on the counter, rubbing his face. He wasn't as annoyed with Brigitte as he tried to be. Bragg had been his only confidante in over a week, and all the detective cared about was facts. Those sporadic, nonsensical facts were insignificant compared to how Lola's void actually made him feel.

"I found her," he said.

Brigitte's back straightened. "I didn't even know you were looking for her."

"I wasn't. Detective Bragg was. I hired him when she left." He shut his eyes and shook his head. "Says she's in Missouri."

"Missouri?" Brigitte asked. "What the hell is she doing there?"

"I have no idea. Other than one hotel charge, there's no other activity on her credit card."

Slowly, Brigitte's eyes widened as she inclined her head toward him. "You tracked her credit card?"

Beau nodded. That was minor in comparison to interrogating Lola's closest friends and family, but he decided to keep that to himself—Brigitte's eyebrows were already halfway up her forehead. "Yes, but there were no charges over the last eight days. Now there's one pending."

"Oh." She crossed her arms, curling her nails into her biceps. "So you're going to go find her?"

"No," Beau said immediately. "I sent Bragg."

Brigitte tilted her head fractionally. "How come?"

Beau didn't know how to answer that. He knew he should just leave her alone, for both their sakes. He didn't want to, though. He was hurt. He still loved her. But above all, he was angry with her. He couldn't walk away, and he couldn't go after her himself. That would tell her she was worth something to him. She was, but Beau wanted to smother that feeling, not nurture it.

Money gave Beau the gift to waste someone else's time instead of his. Bragg would handle everything. He'd bring Lola back kicking and screaming if Beau asked him to. Throw her at his feet. And Beau would get his answers.

"I have to stay close to the office," he said. "I don't have time to chase her down. I just want to know where she is before I decide…"

Their eyes met. Brigitte turned her back to him and put on her oven mitts, but she didn't move beyond that. "What'll you do if you find her?"

73

"I don't know. But I can't let her get away with this."

Brigitte looked over her shoulder at him. "Then why not go yourself?"

"I told you—I have a company to run. That's why I have people like Bragg."

She faced him again, her mitted hands at her sides. "Why waste Bragg's time if Lola isn't worth enough for you to go yourself? Time is your most valuable resource, but your money and energy are equally precious. She's bleeding you out, Beau. Jesus. Warner says he's never seen you this distracted. Just let this thing go."

Lola had been a strain on him one way or another since he'd found her again—yet knowing her had been rewarding in ways he hadn't anticipated. After his proposition to her to spend the night with him, he'd returned home to Brigitte, who hadn't thought it was a waste of anything then.

"You were always on board with my plan," he said. "You even said a million was a small price to pay for what I wanted in return."

"Because it was a game, and you needed that win. Her rejection had been a weak spot for you all those years, and you're the strongest person I know. It was never about getting laid." She shook her head. "This isn't a game anymore, Beau. Part of your success has come from your ability to cut deadweight loose the way most people can't. The moment hesitation or indecision creeps in, you're letting emotion get in the way of your sense. She's offered you an exit, and you need to take it."

Beau asked himself if he could go upstairs, go to bed and never think of Lola again. Bragg wouldn't care either way. He'd walk out of the airport right now, so long as he got paid. Lola and Beau had both hurt each other, but the score would never feel even. How long could it go on? He didn't know, but he couldn't forget her. He hadn't in ten years, and he wouldn't ten years from now. He had to confront her. A small part of him wondered if she wanted him to find her. If she'd made that one credit card charge hoping he'd follow it.

"Can we drop this already and eat some lasagna?" Brigitte asked, sighing as she pulled the oven open.

"Why?"

She slid the dish out and set it on the stove. "Because I'm hungry, and this discussion isn't—"

"No," he interrupted. "Why do I need to take this exit she's given me?"

Brigitte rolled her eyes, removing the oven mitts. "I don't want to see you get hurt yet again. She's put you through enough, and she isn't worth it. Clearly, she doesn't even want to be around you."

Beau folded his arms against his chest and leaned back on the counter. Brigitte never wanted to see him get hurt, and that was why she'd hated Lola from day one. Brigitte and Beau had always decided who got close enough to find their well-hidden weak spots. They'd only been teenagers when the car accident had killed their parents. With his dad's death came the news of his affair with Brigitte's mom. It'd been a day—a lifetime— of struggling with hurt and anger, loss and betrayal. Beau didn't think of it much anymore, but it affected how he dealt with others. Until Lola, he hadn't had a good enough reason to let anyone close.

"Maybe it's time we start living in the real world again, Brigitte. Where people get hurt and they fuck up. Then they come out stronger. Didn't we come out stronger after what we went through?"

"Yes, you and I—"

"I mean as individuals," Beau clarified. "Not as a unit. Maybe it made us too strong."

"That's ridiculous." She waved a spatula in his direction. "Who are you right now? You sound like a therapist."

Beau didn't have to be a therapist to see she was deflecting. He wasn't ready to change the topic, though, and that was unlike him when it came to Brigitte and serious issues. Ever since his breakfast-dinner with Dina Winters, he'd been wondering when he'd become so disconnected from people.

"Let me ask you something," he said. "When's the last time you went on a date?"

She looked over at him, her eyes huge. "What?"

"You heard me."

"Since when do you care?"

"Answer the question. Or are you afraid to?"

"I got out with men all the time."

"I mean someone who actually interests you. Not a potential investor or a business contact."

She twisted her lips. "Don't turn this conversation on me. This is about you and your control issues. Letting go of Lola is the best thing—"

"I see." Beau was annoyed with her as usual, but he couldn't help a small smile. "So everything's about you except what you don't feel like talking about?"

"Everything is not about me. You're frustrated with yourself, and you're taking it out on me so you don't have to deal with it." She dug the spatula into the lasagna. "Let's just have a nice dinner and forget the rest until tomorrow morning. After some good food and rest, you'll see I'm right as usual."

Beau's smiled eased. He'd been supporting Brigitte financially for a long time, but she was the one who took care of him. He'd never asked for it—he didn't even need it. Because it wasn't for him. She did it for herself. "I'm not enough for you, Brigitte. This, us—it's not enough."

She cut squares into the lasagna, the utensil methodically hitting the bottom of the glass dish. "I don't know what you're talking about. You just want me to leave you alone."

"You could be happy, but you choose not to be. You're afraid if you lose me, you won't have anything at all."

She stopped moving, kept her profile to him. "And you're an expert on what I need? You wouldn't even know me if I didn't force you to all the time. You think money is the answer to everything, including me. I'd bet you were the same with Lola. If a problem can't be fixed with a check, all of us are shit out of luck where you're concerned."

Anger surged through Beau, but it died out just as quickly, as if it'd been a conditioned response. He didn't like Brigitte's assumption he valued his money more than Lola, but that didn't mean it had no merit. "I'm not claiming I've been good at any of this. Boyfriend, brother or even friend. Yes, sometimes I send Warner in my place—because I trust him to give you what I can't."

She shook her head. "I don't even know why you're bringing him into this."

"Yes, you do. You're only blind or stupid when you want to be." Beau looked hard at her, the only person he'd ever felt really close to before Lola. Brigitte was more family to him than his own mother. Even with her avoiding his eyes, he could sense her terror. Any time Beau had to leave, whether it was for a business trip or when he moved to the hotel to get some space from her, she got this way. She didn't think she could do it on her own, but once she stopped clinging to Beau, she'd see that wasn't true. "If you knew what would make me happy, wouldn't you want me to have it?" he asked.

After a moment of silence, she said, "Yes."

"I want the same for you. Look who's standing right in front of you, who's there for you whenever you or I call. It isn't me."

"That's what he gets paid to do. I'm just a nuisance to his boss. He gets stuck dealing with me."

"Maybe in the beginning, but much of the time he spends with you isn't because I send him. He wants to do it."

Brigitte stayed quiet. He didn't believe it'd never occurred to her that Warner loved her or that she could have him if she let herself. But Beau obviously knew less about the women in his life than he realized, especially when it came to love.

When it was clear she had nothing to add, Beau went to leave the room.

"Lola," she said suddenly.

He turned around. "What?"

She looked at him finally. "You said if I know what would make you happy, I should tell you. That's what love is, right? Your happiness over my own?"

"Neither of us is happy, Brigitte. Can you honestly tell me this is the life you want? You living here, keeping house, while I work myself to death?"

She shuddered, but her expression didn't change. "You're the only person I have." Her voice was soft. "I don't know how to be without you."

"Warner could be the best thing that's ever happened to you, but you'll never know if I'm in the way."

"And what about Lola? You're going to send a complete stranger after her when she's alone in the middle of the country? I don't understand your fascination with her, but I don't need to. I see you're going crazy without her." She took a deep breath as if it'd required effort to speak that much.

Beau's eyes were dry. He blinked, the first time since she'd started talking. It was the last thing he'd expected to hear from her, but if one thing had always remained true, it was that she loved him even more than she did herself. She just rarely showed it in a non-destructive way.

"You think I should go after her," Beau stated.

"I don't want you to." She held his gaze, also unblinking. "That's how I know you have to."

Chapter Ten

Beau pulled into a parking spot and rubbed his eyes with tense fingers. After a sleepless night at LAX and hours of flying and driving, he still didn't know what the fuck he was going to say to get the information he needed. He got out and shut the door behind him. It'd been daylight when he'd left Los Angeles, but it was almost evening now. The parking lot was dark with storm clouds. The Moose Lodge's exterior could almost pass for a cozy hotel, except that the buzzy glare of its neon sign gave it away as something seedier. The word *Vacancy* was lit underneath it. He hated to think of Lola here by herself, in this slow-life Missouri town, where there was an unwelcome chill in the air.

Across the street, a man in hunter-green camo pants leaned against the wall of a liquor store, watching Beau. A cigarette dangled from his lips. He could've easily been one of Hey Joe's beer guzzlers, the ones

Beau'd seen leering at Lola as she'd wound through two-top tables, her effortless confidence drawing eyes.

Men like that and places like this had gone round and round in Beau's mind the last nine days, a haunted carousel with Lola trapped in the center. The homeless man from the gas station was always on it, and the guy across the street looked eerily similar to him. Him, with his hands on Lola while Beau had stood there, helpless.

Through the gas station's glass door, Beau watched Lola approach, her purse swinging in her hand. The corners of her pressed-together lips curved slightly upward, as if it was a real effort not to smile. In the split second before she pulled open the door, her movements were airy and light, like a woman—he hoped—in love.

Beau would've shouted at her to run if he hadn't thought startling the cagey man who held a gun to Beau's head would earn one of them a bullet.

She breezed in and stopped dead.

"I told you, there isn't a single thing in my car." Beau had been trying to convince the man to stay inside with him instead of going out there, where Lola was. She'd come to them anyway. Beau attempted a discrete but firm jerk of his hand in her direction.

He pleaded with her however he could—with a quick glance, with a stiffening of his body. She should've been far away from there. Leave. Go.

She didn't move an inch. Beau sent the man on a hunt for his wallet as a distraction.

Leave. Get the fuck out of here.

She didn't budge, but cried out, "I have it," and the gun was no longer on Beau.

Beau'd barely slept on his one-way flight out of LAX. After talking to Brigitte, he'd called Bragg to stop him from getting on a plane, but the Midwest storm had done it for him. The detective'd been at the airport for two hours trying to get to Missouri. Beau took his place, waiting out the snow, every passing hour another chance for Lola to slip back into the night. When he couldn't take another minute of that, he demanded a flight that would get him closest to this little lodge in the Missouri mountains. He'd flown into Dallas and driven his rental car eight hours. In the meantime, the storm had mostly passed.

Beau walked up to the front office's glass door and stood just outside of view. That memory of the gas station was always too ready, too easy to call up. Beau still hadn't figured out why he was there. He'd know when he saw her. He just needed to lay his eyes on her again—that was step one.

A potbellied, balding man sat at the check-in desk, a phone lodged between his ruddy cheek and his shoulder while he pounded on a computer keyboard. He said something into the receiver and slammed it down.

Almost immediately, a girl came out of the back, her blonde ponytail swinging. She furrowed her eyebrows, put a slender hand on his shoulder and pointed to something on the screen. The lines in his forehead eased as the splotches on his cheeks became less angry. They smiled at each other, and he stood and left the room.

Enter Beau. He straightened his suit jacket and smoothed his palm over his styled hair. He still needed a haircut, but at least he looked presentable today. Bells chirped against the glass door when he walked in, a jingle to announce him. The girl, no older than eighteen or nineteen, looked up and froze.

"Hi." Beau forced a smile and leaned an elbow on the counter. "How are you?"

"Fine." The word barely disturbed her parted lips.

Neither of them spoke a moment. He didn't get this kind of thing much anymore—the curious, innocent-lust look she was giving him. The women he spent time with had already had their rose-colored glasses removed by someone. He glanced at the monitor and back at her.

"Oh." She jumped into action, clasping the computer mouse in her hand. "You need a room?"

"Actually, no," Beau said, still smiling, still leaning.

She looked up. "No?"

"Well, sort of. I'm hoping you can help me out—what's your name?"

"Uh." She checked over her shoulder. "Matilda?"

"Nice to meet you, Matilda. I'm Beau." He should've been an actor. Or a detective. A story was already brewing inside him, a warm stew to go down easy. "My wife is staying here on business." He declared it—no question about it. Men in bespoke suits did not just wander into motel lobbies and tell lies. "Tonight's our anniversary. She thought she'd have to spend it alone."

"That's strange," the girl said. "We don't get a lot of business types out here, not like Springfield or Harrison. Even then, companies usually book at the Best Western in town." She pointed behind Beau as if he could see from where he stood.

Beau glanced over her head at the backdoor and absentmindedly straightened his tie. "Well, the point is—I drove a long way to see her. To surprise her."

Matilda beat her palm once against her chest. "Really?" she crooned. "That is so romantic."

"I know." Beau kept a smirk from his face. "Here's the thing, Matilda. I don't know which room she's in."

Her face fell except for one blonde eyebrow, which rose. "Oh?"

Beau could almost taste his anticipation. Within moments, he'd be standing in front of Lola's door, and she wouldn't even know it. He'd worried, as he'd driven, that she wouldn't be there anymore, that she'd only stayed one night. But his doubts were gone now. He could sense her there, nearby, unprotected, unsuspecting. Caught in her own trap. "If you could just get me a key to her room—"

"I can't give you that." Terseness clipped Matilda's words, made her back rod straight. "That's illegal."

Illegal? Did this girl think she was in an episode of *CSI: Missouri?* Beau blinked slowly at her. "Not if she's my wife."

"Um, yes, even if she's your wife. Why can't you call her cell phone?"

"I told you, it's a surprise." Beau sounded almost sulky. He envisioned Lola slipping out the backdoor again, right through his fingers just as he closed them around her. So he was no detective. But a starry-eyed teenage girl was no seasoned negotiator. "All right, the key is a lot to ask. I'll just take her room number."

She shook her head.

"What's your objection?" Beau asked.

"It's wrong. How do I know she's actually your wife, and you're not some stalker?"

"I'll leave my wallet and ID here with you. I can get it on my way out."

"You're leaving tonight?"

"That's the plan."

She wrinkled her nose. "Why, if your wife is here?"

"I'm taking her with me."

"But…she has her work thing—"

Beau's nostrils flared. His negotiation skills were better suited to businessmen than stubborn, inquisitive teenagers. He'd once had a good laugh with a subordinate whose fifteen-year-old daughter had seen a picture of daddy's boss and called Beau a 'total hottie.' He plastered on a smile and inclined a little further over the counter. "Matilda, let me ask you something—do you have a boyfriend?"

Her mouth opened and closed. "Not anymore."

"He dumped you."

"How'd you know?"

"Because I've met enough women like you to know how it works. Pretty girls come and go, but it's the ones who're smart *and* pretty who catch shmucks like me off guard." Beau shrugged. "We're intimidated by girls like you, so we screw it up."

She blushed, looking down at the desk. "My dad says that too."

"He sounds like a smart man. My wife—she's one of you." Beau didn't have to reach far there. Lola stunned men, and she was sharp in a way most people weren't, even without logging much time on a college campus or facing a boardroom of Harvard MBAs daily.

But that kind of smart could get you into trouble too. After Beau, Lola should've run home and cried onto Johnny's shoulder like most girls would've. Her life with Johnny never would've been the same, but it would've been safe. Stable.

That wasn't Lola, though. She'd picked a dangerous path instead, willingly entering the ring with a man who had the means—and now an ironclad motive—to bring her down for good if he chose to.

"I've been to hell and back for her," Beau told the girl. "But every time I see her face, I'm reminded why I do it. Help me out, Matilda. I just want to see the expression on her face when I walk into her room. She'll light up with pure *shock*."

Matilda's eyes had grown big and watery, her shoulders slumped with longing. Done deal. He held out his palm for the keycard.

She straightened up, though, pressed her lips together. "I'm sorry, sir," she said, not sounding the least bit sorry. "I legally can*not* give you that information."

Beau dropped his hand on the counter with a slap. This was bullshit. Bragg could've hacked her computer two times over by now. Beau had one negotiation tool she didn't, though, and it was bulletproof. "How much?"

She tilted her head, looking utterly confused. "How much what?"

He hadn't noticed how quick he was to resort to money until he'd done it to Lola's mom in exchange for information. It was beginning to bother him a little, like a dull cramp in his side. It had upset Lola too. He knew, even when she didn't mention it.

The portly man came through the backdoor and waddled over to them. "What's going on, Matty?"

"Dad, this man is asking for a guest's *room key*."

Beau cleared his throat. What was happening to him that he couldn't crack a teenage girl? But at least going up against another man put him back in his comfort zone—because man to man, fortune favored the alpha. "Not a guest," Beau said. "My *wife*. And I don't like being kept from her like this. Do yourself a favor and give me her room number. It'll save you a lot of hassle."

"Calm down, sir," he said. "No need to overreact."

"Overreact?" Beau curled a hand into a fist. "I drove all the way from Dallas to surprise her. That's eight goddamn hours. If I call her, it'll ruin everything."

"She's your wife?" the man asked. "Let me see your license. The names match, we won't have an issue."

Beau refrained from rolling his eyes. His wallet burned a hole in his suit jacket, but showing them his

ID with a name that didn't match hers could mean the end of the conversation. "Well, actually, I don't have my license on me—"

"Didn't you say you drove here?"

"Right. Yes. Sometimes I forget it, though." Beau slid his wallet out. He'd be needing it anyway. He made a show of looking through it, keeping it close to his chest. "That's what I thought. I left it at home. All I have in here is cash." Beau looked up. "Plenty of it."

Both of them shook their righteous heads. "Not going to help you here," the man said.

Beau put his wallet away and leaned his elbows on the counter. "Look. Her name is Lola Winters. Just look her up."

Matilda typed with agonizing slowness. She cocked her head at the computer screen. "What'd you say the first name was?"

"Lola." The look on Matilda's face told Beau something was amiss. It occurred to him that Lola had a reason to stay hidden—him. And he wasn't supposed to know her real name. He added, "It could also be under Melody."

"Here she is."

"Seriously?" Beau asked, taken aback. Confident as he'd been, the news still hit him right in the chest and sent his heart racing with excitement.

"Yeah." The man had been watching over Matilda's shoulder, and he looked up from the computer screen. "You sound surprised."

Beau covered his ass with the biggest smile he had—and it was genuine too. In no time at all, he'd lay his eyes on that black, shiny hair, those big, lying blue eyes. "I'm just eager to see her. Very, very eager."

"I remember her," Matilda quipped. "Checked in last night because of the storm. She didn't mention anything about work."

"That's great," Beau dismissed with a deep inhalation. "Which room? I have flowers in the car, and they need—"

"Oh, no." She shook her head at the computer, her eyebrows triangled in the center of her forehead. "She already checked out."

His heart stabbed him right in the chest, that fickle motherfucker. Bragg had warned him about this—people on the run rarely spent two nights in one spot. But Beau had convinced himself that on some level, Lola wanted him to find her. That maybe, somehow, she wasn't really on the run. She was just drifting. "When?"

"This afternoon, right after the storm let up. Not too long ago. That's weird she didn't mention it to you, especially since she had to work today. What'd you say she does, anyway?"

Beau closed his eyes. He pictured her running away from him through Middle-American wheat fields, her head over her shoulder as she smiled, waved at him. *Ha. Gotcha.* Not knowing where she was had been torture, but just missing her by a few hours was almost worse. If he'd flown to Dallas right when he'd arrived at the airport. If he'd driven twice as fast.

"Did she leave a note?" he asked evenly. "Anything behind?"

"I didn't check her out, but I haven't seen—"

"How about lost and found?"

The girl looked up at her dad.

"Why don't you just call her?" he suggested, watching Beau carefully. "Maybe she went back home or moved to another hotel in the area."

Beau opened his mouth to make his demands. He wanted to speak to whoever'd checked her out. To see surveillance footage. To check the room she'd stayed in for clues. He took a deep breath and walked outside, leaving behind two suspicious expressions. With the time difference, he'd lost two hours between California and there, and it was almost six o'clock at night.

Beau extracted his cell phone from his suit pocket, cringing as if it were painful. He called Bragg and spoke first. "She's gone. Are there any new charges?"

"Not since last night."

"Check again." Beau ignored the detective's sigh and waited on the line. He could still catch her, no matter where she was. If she was driving, he would fly. If she moved fast, he would move faster.

"Nothing, boss," Bragg said into the phone. "You going to stay out there or come back?"

Beau hung up the phone and stared at the black screen. He didn't know where to go from here or if he could go through this again another night. How the fuck could she do this to him? Toy with him this way? He purposely chose not to see the irony in the situation.

He needed to think—to be in a clean, uncluttered place, alone with his thoughts—and to sleep. He'd stayed at The Ritz-Carlton in St. Louis before. He wasn't sure how far it was. There had to be a nearby city with something upscale. But Lola had stayed at the Moose Lodge last night, and suddenly, feeling close to her seemed more important.

He returned to the front office. "I'm sorry if I seemed angry," he said and, to his surprise, he meant it. By not giving Beau information, the young girl had been protecting Lola. No matter how mad he was, Beau could only hope everyone else Lola had encountered so far had done the same. "It's just, my wife—" He practically choked on it. *My wife.*

"Poor thing. You can't even spend a night without her," the girl said—alone again, a hopeless romantic again. "Are you going to be all right?"

Beau nodded. He took his wallet out once more. "Can I get a room for the night?" he asked, holding out his credit card.

She withdrew as though he'd just sneezed on it. "I don't know."

"Please," he said, too exhausted for anything other than begging.

She sighed and took it. "Oh, all right."

"Any room is fine."

She shrugged. "They're all the same, unless you want to be by the icemaker or something."

"Any room is fine," he repeated.

He took his key, then crossed the street to the liquor store. The man in camo was gone. Beau bought the most expensive Scotch they had, a brand he'd never heard of and didn't plan on remembering.

He returned to his room at the Moose Lodge, where there was no minibar, no luxury showerhead, not even a robe. He sat on the edge of the bed with a drink in his hand and stared at a crack in the wall that ran out from behind the midsized TV. There'd been many cracks throughout his life, but very few the last ten years. Money had a way of smoothing them over.

When would she stop? How far would he go? There was a finish line. An edge. There had to be. He couldn't follow her to the ends of the earth and keep his sanity. Selfishly, he hoped at some point she'd run herself into a corner. When she did, he'd be there—right behind her, right in front of her.

The pillows were lumpy, the bathroom lacking in toiletries, the vending machine broken. And except for the fact that almost having her and losing her again felt as if he'd dropped his heart a short distance and fractured it—he was fine at that motel that was not The Ritz-Carlton.

Chapter Eleven

Lola was engrossed in her fifth conversation of the last hour, except that she hadn't said a word. She sat on the terrace of Café Du Monde surrounded by people who'd unknowingly let her into their lives for a few minutes here and there. The family of four to her right had stopped in New Orleans for *beignets* on their drive home from Disneyworld. The little girl wore a Minnie Mouse hat with an oversized red bow that matched her sunburnt nose. The boy's T-shirt, with *Florida* written in Disney lettering across the chest, was also colorfully decorated with food stains.

Lola sipped her second *café au lait*. She'd also heard a French couple's flowering and heated conversation behind her. She couldn't understand or even see them, but she'd imagined their quarrel would catapult them into each other's arms before the night's end.

Her table was like the center of the world that hour, with tourists from all different places to her left and right, in front of and behind her—sitting, drinking, eating, conversing and then leaving to give their table to the next group.

Being as caught up as she was in what was happening around her, she'd almost forgotten she herself was one of them until someone spoke to her.

"I was beginning to think being alone around here was a crime."

Lola glanced over at the nice-looking man at the next table. "It might be," she said. "But I wouldn't know since it makes quick getaways easy."

His answering chuckle was deep and throaty. A piece of his black hair flapped as a breeze passed over them. He held open a hand. "This is risky sixty seconds in, but I'll take the chance. Join me for a pastry?"

His brown eyes matched her milky coffee. The lines around them crinkled with an inviting smile. The last two days had been the regular driving, eating, sleeping and sightseeing. She'd spent more time alone on this trip than she ever had in L.A., but she was only lonely when she thought of Beau. She smiled back at the man. "Thank you, but I'm happy here."

"All right." He dropped his elbow onto the table. "Are you a local too?"

"No." Lola turned in her chair slightly to see him better. "I thought only tourists came here."

"Myth. I've been eating beignets for years, and unfortunately for my figure," he patted his stomach, "I never grow tired of them."

Lola grinned, understanding all too well. Between driving five to ten hours a day and rarely cooking for herself, her pants were getting tight. "It's my only night in New Orleans. As a local—anything I shouldn't miss?"

"Done the French Quarter, I assume?"

Lola nodded. "And a walking tour."

He shrugged. "The best part of this city is…the way it is. I don't know how to describe it. Walk along the Mississippi River or through the streets. To experience New Orleans, just pay attention to what's around you."

"That sounds too easy," Lola joked.

"Existing in the moment? It's harder than you think."

Lola glanced at her hands. The parents returning from Disneyworld had been talking about the workweek ahead of them. A group of girls who'd been sitting near Lola earlier had been reminiscing about New Orleans before Hurricane Katrina. Like most people, Lola was often looking forward or backward while life happened around her.

"What would you say to some exploring?" The man waved at her, bringing her back from her thoughts. "Let me take you around the city, buy you a drink at my favorite spot. New Orleans has a lot of secrets, ones only the locals know. I'll show you how to forget tomorrow and enjoy the present."

Then again, existing in the moment could be overrated. Lola signaled for a waitress, shaking her head at the self-important pick-up line. "No, thanks."

"Are you taken?"

"No."

"Then why not?"

"I'm just not interested." What she didn't say was that even though she was alone, she didn't feel single. A large chunk of her heart still belonged to Beau, and mere weeks wouldn't change that. Lola took out her wallet.

The man held up a hand. "I've got your bill. Go on and enjoy the rest of your night here."

"But—"

"I insist." He leaned over and took the receipt from her table. "If you want to thank me, pay it forward."

Lola wasn't sure what to do other than leave the restaurant. She stopped at a corner market for a new pack of cigarettes, having finished the last one somewhere around the Missouri-Arkansas border. Once her trip ended, so would the bad habit she'd started up again. Cigarettes had become a form of comfort, reminding her of her early days at Hey Joe, when she was off drugs and alcohol completely. Smoking had kept her sane. Until Johnny had started to nag her about that too. Lola knocked the pack against her palm, walking along the Mississippi River.

She eventually stopped and rested her elbows on a railing to watch the day fade over the river. She took a drag of the first cigarette from her last pack. She'd decided in the Ozark Mountains that it was time go home to Los Angeles. Tomorrow, she'd start the trip back. She didn't want to be anywhere else.

Ending the trip felt like closing the door on Beau for good, though. Letting go of her anger meant severing any remaining link to him. That was for the best, but the idea made her stomach turn and her eyes water. It was unexpectedly physical, the process of saying goodbye. Even her jaw tingled. It got stronger, prickling down her throat. Without warning, she gagged.

Lola pulled the cigarette away from her face and looked it over. The river water rippled below her. She put a hand over her mouth, the ground suddenly unsteady, as if she were out at sea.

She realized it wasn't thinking of Beau that'd turned her cheeks warm and her palms clammy. But a cigarette hadn't made her this nauseous since she'd sucked down her first one at fourteen. Lola stuck the butt between her lips and pulled out the pack to check for an expiration date. And then it hit her, the reason her mom had been forced to quit smoking twenty-nine years ago. Lola's mouth fell open. The cigarette dropped onto the concrete, scattering ashes at her feet.

Chapter Twelve

Four weeks earlier

Lola removed her new diamond earrings and set them on the bathroom counter. She glanced up at her reflection. Beau was in the doorway, his bowtie hanging around his neck, a shadow of stubble on his jaw. He came up behind her and slid his arms around her waist. "When did you change?" he whispered. "I wanted to watch."

"I never let you watch."

"That doesn't mean I don't."

Lola's heart skipped as he nuzzled her neck. The idea that he'd seen her undress without her permission made her flush. He was a dog—she knew that. He'd treated her like a dog. What made him think he could get away with that—standing just out of sight as she unzipped the long zippers of the dresses he'd bought her, unclipped the stockings of her wasted lingerie, unclasped her heavy, expensive necklaces. "You watched me?" she asked, her breath coming faster.

"Mmm." He moved her hair aside and kissed a spot under her ear. "No. But it's been very tempting."

The thin silk of her robe did nothing to hide the fact that Beau wanted her. It was a blunt reminder of their knee-quivering chemistry, of being owned by him.

He slid his hand down the smooth fabric and cupped her backside. "All night, I couldn't keep my eyes off you." When he spoke, it was into her neck and hair, breath so hot, him so close, she struggled to maintain focus.

She tried to swallow, but her mouth dried, and her pussy got greedy-wet. She put her palms on the counter, bracing herself as she began to slip under his spell. "Stop," she murmured.

"I'm not doing anything." His fingers curled around the meat of her ass, brushing the private underside of her.

She saw herself—breathing through her nose, reddening from the neck up. Beau was also watching, and their eyes met. He moved both hands around to her tummy and pushed his pelvis into her, sending her gasping toward the mirror.

"You hide it well," he said. "Until you don't. You want to fuck as badly as I do."

She would've denied it, but her vocal chords wouldn't cooperate. He roamed his hands down her body, then up the backs of her thighs, and up and up until he was cupping her tits through the silk. He squeezed them, rubbed them, released them to slip his hands inside her robe and put his skin on hers.

"Oh, God," she said, bending over the lip.

"That's it," he said, keeping her breast in one hand as he undid his pants with the other.

Her protest was a moan. She'd been there less than a week, but her body was rubber-band tight, so tight, and she wanted that release. Needed it. She hadn't even touched herself since the last time he'd been inside her—had just slept chastely by his side the last few nights she'd been living there.

It fascinated Lola to see them together that way. Beau's jaw set as he glanced down and back at her. She'd seen that reckless look in his eyes before—the first night, in Beau's lap at the strip club, and many times after that. He always wanted to get inside her with a determination neither of them could fight.

He slid a finger along her slit, then pressed the tip of his cock to it. Neither of them moved. The bathroom lights glared, suddenly blinding. The longer he rested just his head between her folds, waiting, the harder she throbbed around it.

She knew what he wanted. It wasn't enough to give herself over—she had to beg for it, for him to finish her off for good.

"I can feel you getting wet," he said.

Lola shook her head hard, avoiding her own eyes in the mirror. Her knuckles whitened from making fists.

"No?" he asked. "You think I don't know when your pussy's hungry? Feed it. Push back onto me."

"I can't."

"It wasn't a request."

"You can't tell me what to do," she said. "You don't own me that way anymore."

"I was hoping you'd talk back," he slapped her ass, and she inhaled loudly, "just so I could do that."

She dropped her forehead down as sweat beaded on her upper lip. Her skin smarted where he'd spanked her, radiating to her pussy. It was as if her nerve endings only existed in the places Beau touched her.

"You don't know the satisfaction I get from watching you fight yourself," he said. "Do yourself a favor. Give in." He stepped back, removing the pressure from between her legs.

"What're you doing?" she breathed. She didn't want to ask for it, but she sure as hell didn't want him to stop.

"Hold yourself open for me."

Lola hesitated. Beau was as stubborn as her, and he would walk away to teach her a lesson, even if it meant he wouldn't get to fuck her. Lola reached back, still bent at the hip. She bared her soft, slippery lips, gingerly at first, and then wider as her need took over.

"It is perfection, *ma petite chatte*," he said. "When you behave, all I want is to reward you." He returned behind her, lining his cock up again. "Fuck me."

Lola breathed in and out, her head swimming. She readjusted her grip, spread her pussy and pushed back onto him slowly. He had to help her, to work his head in to loosen her up. When her body gave way, Lola slid back, filling herself with him, her mouth becoming impossibly dry.

"Keep going," he said. "And don't look away from me."

All she wanted to *do* was look away. He was playing dirty, making her break her own rules. Lola watched him as she urged her body forward, gliding up his cock, and then back down, slow and awkward. Beau's expression remained smooth as he watched her face, mild amusement in his eyes.

Her bottom lip was between her teeth, her fingers digging into her skin. She was right where she'd wanted to be the last few days and right where she knew she should never have been again.

"You can let go now," he said.

She released herself just as Beau put a hand on her upper back and pushed her down, her nipples hardening against the cool granite. He grabbed her by the hips and thrust all the way in. They both exhaled a sharp, "*Fuck.*"

He didn't waste another second, suddenly insatiable. He took her fast, pushing her farther over the sink with each drive until she was on the balls of her feet. She held onto the faucet.

"I told you to look at me," he said.

She raised her head, and they found each other in the reflection again. This was something she'd never seen—herself, getting fucked by him from behind. It was better than she'd fantasized. His bowtie was still around his neck. Except for his pants, pushed down around his ass, he was fully dressed. He held her hard, went at her hard, his eyes were hard—but none of it in a bad way.

He practically had her off her feet by the time she came, her climax so ready, it was both effortless and raw. He talked her through it—she was so beautiful, he'd needed this so much, had been dying for it.

With her last spasm, she loosened her grip on the faucet. His neck strained, her breasts swayed, his fingers dented her hips as he pulled her into each thrust. Her eyes darted between everything like she'd walked into the middle of a crime scene and couldn't decide where to look first.

Beau smacked her ass, groaned her name like a prayer and touched her everywhere as he came.

Her hand flew to her mouth, reality slapping her across the face. She'd fucked up—with the worst person possible. The enemy. In a matter of seconds, he'd shattered her carefully-constructed walls like they'd been made of porcelain.

"Christ, Lola." Beau ran his hand up and down the silk of her back, admiring her. His Adam's apple bobbed when he swallowed. "You have no idea, the plans I have—"

"Get off me."

His eyes jumped to hers. "What?"

They held each other's stare, still except for the frantic, synced rise-and-fall of their chests.

"You promised," she said, hating that her voice cracked. "Get *off* me."

"Hey—come on." He smiled a little, the smug fucking bastard. "You're going to tell me that was one-sided?"

She looked up at the ceiling. She'd been stupid to think she could actually do this—be this close to him and not ever *once* let her guard down. She'd known if she did, he'd see that weakness and pounce. She'd been right.

"Fuck you," she said. "You couldn't even do this one simple thing you promised me."

He slid out of her, stepping back. "This has been anything but simple," he said, pulling his pants up quickly, tucking himself into them. "It's goddamn torture following your rules. There's nobody else I'd let get away with that bullshit."

She turned to face him, her robe whispering around her hips. She pulled it closed around her with trembling fists. "Bullshit? It's *bullshit* for me to ask for a little time to recover after what you put me through?"

He ran both hands over his hair. His smile was completely gone, at least, replaced with a solemn frown. "Jesus. I didn't realize this was such a big deal. I thought you were—I don't know. Playing around. Teasing me."

Lola clenched her jaw against a wave of tears. She had to make a choice—break him or leave. Otherwise, she'd never be anything but a pawn to him, and their relationship would never be anything but a game. "I thought I could do this. I thought I could play, but I'm out of my league here."

He shook his head, his drawn eyebrows wrinkling his forehead. "What are you talking about?"

"This isn't working." She took a step forward. "I'm leaving."

He blocked her path. "Like fuck you are."

"Give me one reason why I shouldn't." She looked up at him. "Why would I stay?"

He scoffed and held his arms open. "All of this. The last few days. I make one mistake, and you're going to walk away? Like we didn't fight like hell to get here?"

"I have to. If you don't respect me by now, you never will. I came back for you. I swallowed my pride. Every day I stay despite my better judgment. I asked one thing of you—keep your hands to yourself. Just for a little while."

"You're right. I'm sorry."

Lola flinched. It was unexpected—the sweet kind of desperation on his face she wasn't used to seeing. Her plan might actually have been working the last few days, small and subtle changes right before her eyes.

"I didn't understand why this meant so much to you," he continued, "but I do now."

She shifted on her bare feet. "How do I know you aren't just saying that?"

He reached up and hesitated, his hands hovering over her cheeks. When she realized he was waiting for permission, she nodded slightly. He touched her face with his palms, as if committing it to memory, then took hold of her shoulders. "Don't go." He pulled her closer to him, and she went. He kissed her forehead and the bridge of her nose. "Be mad. Scream at me. Make me pay. But don't go—that would be the worst. All right, Lola? I want you here. I really want you here."

Her posture eased a little. He did love her, she knew it, clung to it. She'd screwed up huge, but it would have to be a lesson learned. Staying alert wasn't enough.

She had to be vigilant around him. She had to monitor every touch, every look, from somewhere outside herself.

"Let's just go to bed," she said quietly, looking to the side.

He released his grip a little. "Thank you."

He walked out of the bathroom, but she stood there a second longer. Her anger drained with the blood from her face. She hadn't taken birth control in days. That month's pack had been in her purse when it was stolen, and she hadn't thought to bring the rest from her apartment. Not once had it occurred to her that she might need it.

Lola straightened her robe and combed her fingers through her hair before leaving the bathroom. She was fairly certain birth control didn't leave your system for a while. Either way, nothing would happen—because it couldn't. It just couldn't. She had enough to worry about as it was, and anything more would surely be the last straw for her. It was hard to imagine anything beautiful could come from this ugliness anyway.

Chapter Thirteen

Present day

Beau left the Moose Lodge behind in the backwoods of Missouri to be closer to an international airport. He didn't know where Lola would go next, but this time he'd be ready. Beau found sitting still one of his greater challenges, but he worried if he went up, she'd go down, left or right.

Two days he waited, during which his assistant arranged for him to meet with a couple startups, both of which impressed him. They were green but viable, and more surprisingly, unaffected. The big-city entrepreneurs he normally met with were eerily familiar to him—they were versions of Beau before he'd hit it big. They had dark circles under their eyes all the time and consumed caffeine like water. They were always trying to stay ahead of the game, but sometimes that cost them.

When Bragg called, Beau was visiting a major hotel in Memphis. He held his Entrepreneurs in Tech conference in Los Angeles every year, but it'd occurred to him sometime over the last couple days that he and his partner had been focused on California too long. There was talent everywhere—even Tennessee. An entire nation waited to be discovered.

That didn't mean, for even a moment, Lola was far from his mind. Beau kept his eyes up all the time, wondering if he might turn the corner and run right into her.

Beau held up a finger to the hotel's sales manager when he saw Detective Bragg's name on the screen of his cell phone. "Excuse me, I have to take this."

"Louisiana," Bragg said into the phone before Beau'd even spoken.

Beau put his hand on his hip. "She's there?"

"I woke up to a pending charge at a gas station in New Orleans. Called around the immediate area and found a motel with a Lola Winters staying there—you might have to write a check for that info."

"I might or I will?"

"What's a few hundred more bucks?"

Nothing to him. But he'd developed this strange habit, this rapid reach for his wallet. Beau valued his fortune, having been without it most of his life, but the look people got when they had a chance at easy money—it was seductive.

The lights in the conference center got brighter, or so it felt. He blinked a few times, already moving in the direction of the exit. He pulled the phone away briefly to tell the woman showing him the space, "My assistant will be in touch."

Bragg coughed into the phone. "I'll e-mail the details right now."

"How far is New Orleans from me?"

"Six hours in the car, four in the air, minus boarding."

"I'm getting on the road now."

"I got a feeling today's the day, want to know why?"

Satisfaction tinged Bragg's voice, something Beau'd been waiting on for a while. "Why?"

"Every day since we got her real name, I've been hunting car salesmen, trying to find one who worked with a Melody Winters. Those guys love their cash upfront. Well, goddamn if I didn't put a bullet in one's ass this morning. She's driving a red Lotus Evora. Got the plates too. How's that for you? She may be flying under the radar, but in a car like that, doesn't exactly seem like she wants to stay hidden."

For the third time in two days, Beau tasted victory. It was even sweeter now that he knew how she was traveling and what to look for. He would've guessed black for her, but he liked the red. A lot. "Good work, Bragg." Beau hesitated. "But you didn't really shoot anyone, did you?"

The detective guffawed into the phone. Beau was afraid it'd devolve into another coughing fit, but Bragg just said, "Not today, kid," and hung up.

Beau decided to drive to Louisiana. Behind the wheel, at least he'd have some control. Airports were too sluggish, even when they were fast-paced, the stale air like sludge for hurried travelers.

Why had she chosen to go south now? It was an unusual move, and to keep going across country, she'd have to come up again eventually. Unless she went west, and that would put her back toward Los Angeles. Home. He wanted to get to her before then. He fantasized about catching Lola in the act, making eye contact with her amidst the Bourbon Street crowd, sending a Sazerac to her table as he watched from the bar, standing inches behind her as she took in a sunset behind the three-steepled St. Louis Cathedral. As if her reaching L.A. before he'd caught her meant she'd be able to deny this'd ever happened.

In the car, his assistant called. "They're ready to finalize the VenTech acquisition," she said. "I can arrange a meeting first thing in the morning."

They'd had to move quickly to prepare an offer for VenTech's founder while its future was bleak, and before anyone else could. Beau had known this was coming, and even though he was the only one who really cared about the buyout, he couldn't help cursing the timing. "Make sure Larry's there," Beau said. "I'm not sure I'll make it in time."

"I already looked at flights," she said. "Getting you into LAX by tomorrow morning shouldn't be an issue."

Beau looked up from the road. Small, white-bellied birds flapped across the sky in formation. Once Bolt Ventures had put the finishing touches on the paperwork, it would only be days before Beau could go to George Wright with an offer—a laughable one, but one Wright couldn't afford to turn down. But that would mean getting on a plane tonight and missing another chance to find Lola.

"I'm the one who wanted this," Beau said. "I should be there."

"Probably, but…"

"But what?"

His assistant didn't respond. He knew where she was headed, but he'd bitten her head off enough times when she'd suggested unloading his work to others.

Beau uncurled his fingers from the steering wheel, splaying them, an invitation. "You think they can manage without me."

"You can't be everywhere all the time, Mr. Olivier."

"Sure I can, thanks to modern technology."

"You can videoconference. Although, that doesn't mean you should. It sounds like you have more important things going on."

"All right." Giving in to others was physical for him, a tightening and loosening of his shoulders, an anxious nod of his head. "Fine. If I'm free, I'll video in. If not, they'll have to proceed without me."

"Okay—"

"But make sure Larry calls me before they make any—"

"I'll take care of it, Mr. Olivier. Just enjoy your vacation."

"I'm not on—"

The line went dead, the first time she'd ever cut him off that way. He set his phone down, envisioning everyone in the office break room, celebrating his absence. He doubted that, though. Beau could be hard, but he was a good boss and a good man to work for—he knew that. Maybe that was why they all seemed to think he needed time away.

He shifted in his seat, the road out his windshield narrowing into the horizon. He thought about e-mailing his assistant and asking her to send detailed minutes of the meeting directly after, but he let it go.

Lola had mentioned more than once his frustrating devotion to work. She'd wanted more of his attention than she got. Well, she had it all now.

◆ ◆ ◆

Beau spotted the New Orleans motel a second too late, and his tires shotgun-shrieked against the pavement when he slammed on his brakes. He veered across oncoming traffic into the parking lot. Lola wasn't far now. She might not be in her room, but he had all evening to find her. They'd been playing this game for too long—it had to end. They would argue, that was unavoidable—he was angry. Seeing her again would test his control. But then what?

Beau entered the front office chest first, his authority unmistakable. "I'm looking for a woman who checked in here earlier."

The long-nosed, pimple-faced clerk was unimpressed. "We get a lot of those—women."

Beau flattened his hand on the counter. "My associate called and spoke to someone. Was it you?"

"Your associate?" He looked over Beau's shoulder, then his own. "Uh, it wasn't me."

"Is there anyone else working?"

"Yeah, but he's on his break for another twenty minutes."

"Fine. Her name is Melody Winters. Check your system."

The man blinked once slowly before turning to the computer. His mouse clicked, his fingers tapped the keyboard. He shook his head. "I don't see her…"

"But I was told that she's here."

The clerk raised his eyebrows. "Hmm. Uh…"

"What?"

"What'd you say the first name was?"

"Melody."

"Oh." He shook his head. "Nope."

Beau rolled his eyes. He inched his hands closer to the computer, tempted to jerk the screen in his direction. "How about Lola?"

"Oh." The man nodded. "Yep."

"She's here?" Beau's frustration yielded to relief. "Which room?"

"I can't—"

JESSICA HAWKINS

"Money. I have it. You can have it. For your cooperation." Beau almost cringed, barely able to form a full sentence. He wanted to be better, to do this the right way, but he couldn't help himself. He'd come too far, was too close, to start following some ambiguous set of rules. He fumbled in his jacket pocket for his wallet, pulled out three crisp one-hundred-dollar bills. "You can come with me if you don't trust me. Keep my wallet as collateral. Whatever. Just give me the room number."

The man looked from the money to Beau to the door behind him. He slid the cash toward himself on the counter and pocketed it. He wrote something on a slip of paper and held it out.

Before Beau could take it, the clerk pulled it back and whispered, "I never gave this to you."

"Fine."

"Destroy it when you're done."

"Give me the fucking paper."

The man's eyes widened. He handed it over.

118.

Beau went to room 118 and knocked. He sniffed, stuck his hands in his pockets. So much for a thought-out, specially-tailored plan. He banged on the door until it opened to reveal a short, gray-haired woman.

"Who are you?" he demanded.

She scowled. "You knocked on *my* door."

"I'm looking for my—my girlfriend...my wife..."

"Well, which is it?" the lady asked.

"She told me she was in room 118."

"Harold," the woman called behind her without removing her eyes from Beau.

"I'm not here to bother you," Beau said, holding up his palms. After a nostril-full of air, he said, "I'm just looking for my wife—have you seen her by any chance? Dark hair, slim, tall, blue eyes, shiny hair—"

"Oh—shiny hair," the woman exclaimed. "How on earth does she get it so shiny?"

"What?"

"I know exactly who you're talking about. Lola."

"Right," Beau said so loudly, the woman jumped. "That's her. Is she in there?"

"In *here*?" The woman shook her head. "What a doll. What an angel. You are a lucky man."

"I'm a desperate man," Beau said. "Where is she?"

She tapped a finger on her chin. "Gone, I think." Her eyebrows knit. "She didn't mention anything about a husband."

His heart dropped. It was impossible. He wasn't even in the room, and the walls seemed to be closing in around him. Somebody had to be responsible for putting him through this shit hour after fucking hour. He would wring that person's neck for it—the clerk, this woman, Bragg. Lola. He steadied himself against the doorframe. "Gone? When did you see her?"

"Well, earlier this afternoon, Harold and I were checking in at the front office right over there," she pointed to where Beau had just been, "when this girl comes in behind us. See, Harold and I had some trouble with our trailer this morning, so we had nowhere to sleep and not much cash on us."

Beau's face was getting hot. He rolled his lips together to keep from hurrying her along.

"We were trying to work out a deal when Lola taps me on the shoulder and says she paid for two nights—"

"Word for word," Beau interrupted. "What'd she say?"

"Ah. Um, let's see. She introduces herself and goes, 'I was thinking of canceling my second night, so why don't you take it instead?' I ask if she's sure, and she says something like, 'I'm sure. I just got some news, and it's time for me to move on.' The darling girl, she didn't charge us a thing and was out of the room in ten minutes."

Beau was shaking his head. "No. That's bullshit."

"You're a bit pale," she said. "You want to sit down? My husband's right inside, so don't get any ideas—"

He walked away, got in his car and stared forward. Now, it was the roof that was falling on him. Lola had to have known he was coming somehow—to have done this on purpose. Revenge. Wasn't it? She couldn't know, though—it wasn't like she'd violated his privacy like he had hers, scouring his credit card statements, tracing his phone calls, hunting for clues. He slammed his palms into the steering wheel. He did it another time, honking the horn.

"What the fuck, Lola? What are you doing to me?" He took a deep breath. "Enough is enough. I'm done with this. I'm done looking for you in the corners of the earth. I've had enough."

But he took out his phone and dialed the number he'd already been abusing almost two weeks.

"Let me guess," Bragg answered. "You're so grateful for my help, you're calling to see where you should send my bonus. I appreciate that, I really do— you got a pen?"

"Have there been any other charges?" Beau asked. "Anything at all."

Bragg sighed heavily. "No, kid. I'm sorry."

"Are you sure there isn't any way she has another card or a cell phone? How'd she get this far without charging more?"

"We've been over this. It's the cash."

Beau looked at his lap. She had run because of him, and she stayed hidden because of him. He'd thought buying her would give him the last laugh, but he sat in his car, unable to even remember the happiness he'd had just a short time ago. And to think there was a time he'd thought he could slice her right out of his life like a bruise from a peach. He'd done this to himself—and it'd been *deliberate*.

Bragg cleared his throat. "Look, Beau…"

Beau lifted his eyes a little. "What?"

"Maybe it's time to take a break. You've been looking for this girl for a couple weeks now, and you got nothing to hang your hat on." He hesitated. "Thing is, you haven't even told me the reason."

"You want to know why?"

"Guess I should've asked this earlier, but you didn't strike me as the vengeful type—it's not because you want to hurt her, is it? Just that you seem a little strung out."

"No," Beau said flatly. "I don't *want* to hurt her. There are a lot of things I don't want to do, though, like keep chasing her or go home without her."

Bragg grunted. "Could it be that you're in love with her?"

It was such an odd question, even odder coming from Bragg, who never asked why—who rarely strayed from business. Beau didn't answer.

"Don't you have someone you can talk to about this?" Bragg asked. "Brigitte?"

"Brigitte hates any woman who has my attention."

"I don't know anything about that," the detective said, "but I do know this ain't healthy. You've got to let Lola go. I think she wants to be let go."

"I know, it's just that we had these two nights…" Beau said.

Bragg was silent. Beau didn't blame him. It was a weird thing to say. He'd had no one to talk to about this. He wasn't even sure he could count his time with Lola after those two nights—not if she'd been plotting against him the whole time. His heart sank. Maybe that was how she'd felt about *all* of their time together.

"You fell in love with someone in two nights?" Bragg asked. "That's—"

"What, impossible?" Beau laughed grimly and hung up the phone. Bragg had no idea just how possible it was.

He jumped at a noise. The woman from 118 was tapping on his window, motioning for him to roll it down. He opened the door and got out.

"Are you all right?" she asked. "I'm sorry if I was rude about you knocking on my door, but you were in a fit. Still are. You don't look like you should be driving."

"Did she say anything else?" Beau asked. "Anything at all? What was she wearing?"

The woman shook her head. "Jeans, I think. Nothing out of the ordinary."

"Was she in a red car?"

She frowned and reached toward him. After a brief hesitation, she rubbed his shoulder. "I'm real sorry, honey. I wish I knew more. She's a lovely girl. I'd hate to lose her too. Maybe there's some way Howard and I can help you find her."

He searched her eyes, finding warmth that hadn't been there before. He'd barged into that hotel like he'd owned it, demanding things and banging on doors. What the fuck was happening to him? What he had wasn't enough—he had to make people feel small too?

"Why would you help me?" he asked.

She smiled a little. "You seem like a good man who got caught in a nasty web. You have that look about you like you might take off running any second." She shrugged. "You know, Lola did say one more thing on her way out the door that makes me think she might like me to help out."

His ears rang. "What was it?"

"I asked if there was any way we could thank her. She says, 'All I did was pay it forward. If you want to thank me, do the same.'"

Chapter Fourteen

Lola stepped out of the motel shower onto a frayed floor mat and wrapped a towel under her arms. After seven hours of traveling, her shoulders ached. The fluorescent light flickered angrily. She wiped steam from the mirror, her face developing in parts. She looked older. A couple vertical wrinkles between her eyebrows remained even after she'd stopped frowning. Smaller ones were forming at the corners of her eyes. Her hair was longer than she'd ever worn it, the wet ends stuck to her breasts, right above her nipples. She couldn't remember when she'd last had it cut.

Even after a shower, her skin showed indents from the waistband of her pants. She turned sideways and ran her hand over her naked tummy. It was too early to see any change, but she thought she could. On the counter next to her was a stick that looked like a headless toothbrush.

After check-in, she'd made herself watch TV for an hour while drinking water and patiently waiting for her bladder to fill. She didn't want to do it wrong—it was the first pregnancy test she'd ever taken, anyway. She'd peed on it and chanted—*two lines pregnant, one line not.* As if she might forget and have to check the instructions a second time.

They had faded in, two lines, distinct and solid. She'd already known what the verdict would be, so she'd gotten in the shower without making a big thing of it. One night of tossing and turning plus a drive from New Orleans to Houston had been a good amount of time to let the news sink in.

Lola dried her hair with the towel and caught herself smiling in the reflection. She was going to be a mom.

She dropped the pregnancy test in the trash behind the toilet, then reflexively tried to catch it at the last second. Was she supposed to keep it as some sort of souvenir? The thought made her wrinkle her nose. She left it and washed her hands for a third time.

She changed into her pajamas, sat on the bed against the headboard and aimed the remote at the TV, but didn't turn it on. Suddenly, she covered her mouth and giggled into her hand. So the news hadn't actually sunken in—not completely. She kept having giddy, heart-soaring moments where she wanted to run outside and tell someone, anyone, how drastically her life had changed in mere months. That kind of news was hard to keep inside.

Lola stuck her thumbnail between her teeth, checking the clock from the corner of her eye. Her suitcase was by the bed, sleeves, pant legs and bra straps sprouting from all sides. Pregnancy would mean the death of her leather pants, at least for a while. She couldn't imagine chasing a juice-sticky toddler around in them. The pants' last night out had been when she'd met Beau, their stiff creak the only sound as she'd cautiously approached him, both of them lit up by the neon signs in Hey Joe's window.

She and Beau were forever linked now. She wouldn't be able to keep the secret long, nor did she want to. The time would come to tell Beau he was going to be a father. Maybe he didn't want that. Maybe he would be angry. She looked at her fingers, bit at a hangnail. He'd made her sign that contract in the beginning, absolving him of any responsibility should she get pregnant. The thought of having his child had disgusted her then, but now she couldn't drum up a negative feeling about it. If he wanted nothing to do with them, she'd deal with it. She wasn't sure what role she wanted him to play anyway.

It was 7:32 at night on the West Coast, two hours behind Houston. That meant in California time, she was still waiting for her bladder to fill, the pregnancy test placed conspicuously at the edge of the bedside stand.

Lola could only think of one person to share her news with. She wasn't sure how her mother, who hadn't even been happy about her own pregnancy, would take it, but Lola had gone too long without talking to anyone familiar. Any reaction seemed better than none. Lola picked up the phone by the bed and dialed a number she'd never forgotten, even though she rarely used it.

"Hel-*lo*?" Dina asked. Just answering the phone had already annoyed her.

Lola opened her mouth. She'd half expected to get the answering machine since her mom often worked nights at the diner.

"Yeah?" Dina said. "Why you people always calling me a minute after I sit down to dinner? Hello?"

"Mom? It's me, Mom."

"Lola?" There was quick screech in the background. "Hang on, I'm sitting down."

Whenever Lola pictured her mom, it was usually in her uniform—dumping a Styrofoam container on the kitchen counter after a shift, or at the diner, swishing by the booth where Lola sat, her legs hanging over the edge as she colored or did homework. Lola rarely thought of her at home, eating a solo dinner. She wondered if she ate at the kitchen table or on the living room sofa. She used to fall asleep there watching PBS specials like *Andy Williams: Greatest Hits!*

"You there, Lola? I thought you were a telemarketer."

Lola nodded, looking down at her lap. It was comfortingly familiar, that gravelly voice built for hollering out breakfast orders. "How are you?"

"I'm fine. Been worried about you, though."

Lola raised her eyebrows. "Really?"

"Tried to reach you, but that girl at the bar, Veronica, she told me nobody's seen you. Said Johnny didn't phone because he's scared of me. Hasn't returned my call."

"That's because we—did she mention—?"

"You and Johnny are done, yeah. Wouldn't say why, though, not her business."

"Okay. Well, that's not why I'm calling."

"But you know how I feel about Johnny. I been trying to figure out what could've gone wrong. I spoke to him a few months ago, and everything seemed fine."

"It's a long story. We both got sort of…off track."

"Off track? Both of you? Him too?"

"He's not the angel you think he is, Mom."

She grunted. "Maybe not. What about you, though? You getting off track got something to do with the man who came by the diner?"

Her ear tingled, as if Dina's words had physically tickled her. Even though Lola'd gone through so much to get away from him, she hoped that man was Beau. And not because going as far as to track down Dina definitely meant he was unraveling. "Who?"

"Come to think of it, I don't think I got his name." She made a noise like she was thinking, coming up short with ways to describe him. "He was wearing a suit."

"When? What did he say?"

"Almost a week ago. He was looking for you."

Lola only realized her hand was flattened on her chest when she felt her heart beating against her palm. "Did you tell him anything?"

Dina laughed in one loud bark. "What would I say? I know less than anyone. He'd have had better luck with Johnny and them."

129

Lola's blood froze. *Johnny and them.* She hadn't thought, in very much detail at least, of Beau going down to Hey Joe and turning the place upside down looking for her. "Have you heard from anyone since?"

"Just when I talked to Veronica. Already told you my whole conversation with her. What's all this about, Lola?"

"Johnny and I—yes, that man has a lot to do with it," Lola said carefully. "He's why I left."

"Where are you?"

"Texas."

"Well, shit, Lola. I know we don't speak, but I'd like to know when you're leaving the damn state. You been gone this whole time?"

"About two weeks." She smiled a little. "I'm seeing so many things, and I've barely scratched the surface. This country is…big."

"So I've heard."

Always with Dina, what she didn't say was louder than what she did. She'd never had the chance to see the country. Too much of her time and money had gone to raising Lola. "Do you ever think about retiring from the diner?"

"Nah. I never had that itch to go anywhere." Dina cleared her throat. "I know you did, though. Before you met Johnny, I didn't think you could stay in one spot for so long."

"I'm coming home, though. I want to."

"Vacation's got to end at some point, right? Couldn't've saved up much bartending. Where you going to live?"

"I don't know yet. But…there's more. The real reason I'm calling—" Lola's stomach churned, her nerves suddenly popping like firecrackers. Lola hadn't been a happy surprise for Dina. This baby couldn't be worse timing for Lola, and she wasn't sure she wanted a child right now. But even if he was the man who'd hurt her, even with the damage he'd caused, there was something intrinsically comforting about it being Beau's. She would carry his baby with pride.

"You know," Dina said when Lola didn't continue, "I love Johnny lots. Think he was good for you. But I think it's for the best, you moving on. At first, I thought you needed to calm down, and he was good at that. Now, though…ah, I don't know what I'm trying to say, just that—maybe I took his side sometimes, and I'm real sorry for that. You're my family, not him." She rushed out the last few words, as if she might lose her nerve before she could say them.

Lola's throat got thick, her mouth full of marbles. It was hard for both of them to come out and say how they felt, admit when they were wrong. "Thanks," Lola said, her eyes watering a little. "You're going to be a grandma."

"You what? Hang on. Damn TV's too loud." The chair scratched against the tile floor again. The TV got louder, then went quiet. "What'd you say?"

"I'm pregnant," Lola said, pronouncing each syllable.

"What I thought you said," Dina muttered.

The line went static-still for a few seconds. In the silence, over and over, Lola thought—*I can do this by myself*. She might have to. She was strong enough. Her mom's disappointment would only steel her for Beau's reaction.

"Who's the daddy?" Dina asked.

"The man in the suit."

"You sure? He made it sound like he hadn't seen you in a while."

"I'm sure." Lola had been over this already. Her last period had ended the same day Beau'd fucked her over the bathroom sink.

Lola thought about explaining it further, but how could she? She wouldn't lie to her mom, but she couldn't tell her the truth—not at this point in time anyway. There were too many intimate, complicated details to her story with Beau, details only she and Beau could ever know or understand. Beau was the only person who'd never judged her for taking that money, and the only one who never would.

"Motherhood's not cut out for everyone, Lola. Look, not saying I regret it, but I wasn't right for the job back then. You sure you want to go through with it?"

Lola's swallowed. She couldn't bring herself to seriously consider abortion, the same way she'd never thought to take a morning-after pill. She'd convinced herself one unprotected night with Beau, whom she'd considered the devil himself, couldn't result in anything positive.

"Yes," Lola said. "I'm on my own, but I can do it. I had a good example."

Dina made a noise like she was trying to get something out of her throat. "That's sweet, but we both know I was no good at the mom thing."

"Yeah, you are." She'd left her mom's house over ten years ago, bitter and determined to do her own thing. A mom who hadn't given Lola much didn't get to tell her how to live her life or shame her for how she chose to make a living. But Dina had been consistent. She'd always had some kind of dinner on the table and had never spent even one night away from the house when Lola was home.

"We fought a lot over my choices," Lola said. "I used to think it was because you were trying to ruin my life. But you were just being a mom."

"I wanted to be around more, believe it or not. When you told me about the stripping, I blamed myself. Thought it was because I did wrong."

"I know." Lola picked at nothing on the comforter. "You did the best you could, and I see that now."

"How far along?" Dina never made apologies for changing the subject when it suited her. "You know the sex?"

"Only five weeks." Every day since Lola'd seen the boy playing in the snow outside the motel, she'd thought of him. He'd made some kind of unshakable impression on her. The strange thing was, she'd been inexplicably drawn to him but hadn't even known she was pregnant at the time. "It'll be a boy. I'm pretty sure."

"Lucky. They're lots easier than little girls." Dina laughed good-naturedly, and Lola giggled along with her.

"Come and see me when you get back? If you need a place to stay..." Dina hesitated. "You know. We'll figure this out. You're not alone, baby."

Lola needed to get off the phone. She wouldn't be able to keep the tears from spilling much longer. Her mom hadn't called her "baby" since she was a teenager, since before she'd announced she was taking a job at Cat Shoppe and it wasn't open for discussion. "I will. Night, Mom."

Lola hung up and dried the corners of her eyes with her sleeves. Her burden was a little lighter knowing her mom would be there for her again.

Her relief was short-lived, though. Now, Lola had her confirmation—Beau was looking for her. She didn't believe he was capable of hurting her, but Lola had purposely tried to drive him to the edge. And if he was there, he'd want her there with him. Lola glanced down at her hands, instinctively spread over her stomach.

Chapter Fifteen

Beau emptied his pockets into a small, circular tray and added his Rolex to the top of the pile.

A stocky security woman by the metal detector waved in the direction of his feet. "Shoes too."

He slid off his Italian loafers and placed them on the conveyor belt. She nodded for him to pass.

On the other side, he put himself back together, tucking his wallet into his jacket, delicately twisting his feet into his shoes. He normally had a shoehorn in his carryon, but it only occurred to him now that he'd packed it away. He'd already held up the line at check-in, unable to find the airline confirmation in his e-mail. It took a phone call to his assistant to remember he hadn't asked her to book anything.

The first flight out of New Orleans to Los Angeles was a redeye. Beau didn't have to wait at the gate long before priority members were invited to board. He sat, his window rain-splattered, the runway misty. He looked away and checked his e-mail. There wasn't enough to keep him occupied.

People filed by him. He actually hoped to get stuck next to someone chatty. Bonus if it was a beautiful woman. Nobody stopped, though, and eventually the cabin doors shut, the engines vibrated to life. A glassy-eyed flight attendant recited her safety speech.

When they were in the air, she made her way down the aisle. "Get you anything, Miss? Sir, would you like a drink? Do you need anything?"

She parked her cart next to his seat. He looked up at her. "Scotch, neat."

"Right away, sir."

She left it on the seatback tray in front of him. The cabin dimmed and went dark, leaving him alone with his drink. He punched on the light above his head and opened the inflight magazine to a random page.

"Ten Midwest Destinations You Can't Miss."

He'd been to three. What about Lola? Had she driven to the St. Louis Arch in her red sports car and tight leather pants? Where did she keep all that cash? Beau looked up at the low ceiling, stretching his legs out under the seat in front of him. If first class was this cramped, he didn't think he'd survive in coach. He leaned into the aisle. "Miss? Hello?"

After a moment, the attendant appeared, bending over to whisper, "Yes, sir?"

"Another Scotch."

"Certainly." She turned away and within a minute, came to refill his cup.

"Leave the bottle," he said.

"I'm sorry, but—"

"I'll pay." He shifted to get his wallet. "How much is it?"

"We aren't allowed, sir. Are you all right? Do you need a barf bag?"

Beau grimaced, leaning away from her as if *she* were about to be sick. "I feel fine. I just don't—fly well." He flew all the time and had never had an issue. Beau took a too-big sip of his drink as the stewardess stood there. He needed a barf bag for his life. He wanted to tell her the story of how a gravely bad decision had rippled through his neatly-packaged world and turned it into shit. Not even thinking about his healthy bank account gave him comfort at that moment. *She* was a woman—maybe *she* could tell him what the fuck he didn't understand about the female gender.

Beau finished the drink and held out his cup. "One more. Then I can sleep."

She looked around the cabin, quiet except for one snoring idiot. She filled his drink to the brim and left.

What a magic trick Lola had pulled, disappearing into thin air, reappearing in the backwoods of Missouri. She couldn't run forever, though. At some point, she'd have to get a job, pay rent or a mortgage, charge things to her credit card like every other living, breathing American. He could wait in the wings, fading into one of her distant memories. He wouldn't pounce until she thought she was safe.

He didn't want to pounce, though, and he didn't want to be a memory. He could picture her now, sleeping next to him in bed, opening her eyes every few minutes as if to check he was still there. What was real, and what had she faked? Lola in his bed, wearing that piece-of-shit nightgown he passionately *hated*.

Beau thumped his head back against the leathery cushion. Everything began to spin. He tossed the magazine into the seat next to him and switched off the light, praying he wouldn't need that barf bag after all.

Face to face with the woman in New Orleans who was paying forward Lola's favor, Beau'd never felt more like he was standing in ruins he'd caused. Lola didn't want to be found. It wasn't that he thought he deserved her anymore. The opposite, in fact. But that'd never stopped him from pursuing anything. He'd negotiated business deals with men even more powerful than him and regularly took on entire boardrooms. Yet the girl in cat ears unraveled him. He would always be weak when it came to her.

This wasn't business. It wasn't a game. Lola wanted him out of her life and after the way he'd treated her, she had every right. The way to love her was to respect what she was telling him, not demand that she do things his way. The couple had paid it forward, and now it was his turn. He could sit and think up a million ways to make her happy, but it wouldn't matter, because she'd only actually left him one option—leave her alone.

The plane's engines hummed him a lullaby, his consciousness circling the drain. He glided his hand over the smooth surface of the seat's armrest. He could still appreciate her skin, the way she wore an evening gown, or had one ripped off. Thighs spread, tits pointed to the moon, firm but soft ass—and all this against the midnight hair on her head, between her legs.

Her eyelids would fall just as she'd catch her orgasm, never fully closing. She watched him watching her. Lola in her dresses, black and gold and peach. Turning her head over her shoulder and making eye contact with him. Smiling in the seat next to him at the theater, her polite applause. On the stage at Cat Shoppe, pirouetting around the pole in pink, arched ballet slippers, legs bowed, arms bent. A female audience member turned to him. "As we begin our descent, please make sure your seatbelt is securely fastened…"

Beau walked out of the strip club into a desert, sand crunching under the soles of his dress shoes as he stepped over fat succulent plants. "Where am I?"

"Local time in Phoenix is 4:05 in the morning. The temperature is sixty degrees."

"I'm not supposed to be here."

"She knows that," said a female voice.

"Who?"

A camera shutter clicked, a light flashed. He squinted across a canyon at a young Lola, four or five years old, as she shielded her eyes from the sun. The horizon rippled.

"How could you not recognize her?" Lola's voice asked from behind him. "Your own daughter?"

He turned around. Lola stood in Beau's kitchen. A little girl clutched her leg. They both wore leotards and ballet slippers, fabric bunched at their ankles. The child's hair was as dark as her mother's, her cheeks flushed pink.

"My daughter?" he asked.

"Isn't that why you're here?" Lola sounded angry. "I don't think you're supposed to be here. You should leave."

"But I've been looking for you." She was trying to leave again. He lunged for her.

"Help," she screamed, backing into a refrigerator. "Somebody help. Hello? Sir?"

Beau woke up to blinding fluorescence. He blinked up at the flight attendant, whose eyebrows were wrinkled with concern. "Sir? Are you feeling okay? We've landed in Phoenix. If you have a connection to make, you should go now."

Beau sat up in his seat. He was sweating through his suit, his hairline damp. Someone had taken his empty glass and raised his tray. He rubbed his face, his stubbly chin. When he blinked, the little girl was there in her bubblegum-colored outfit, a carbon copy of her mother.

He hadn't just lost Lola when he'd hurt her—he'd given up a life with her. Already, memories he'd never get were tormenting him. Beau stood and took his carryon from the overhead bin. The airport was midnight-quiet, Phoenix's dry desert air in his chest, his throat. Choking him.

Chapter Sixteen

Beau straightened his tie and exited the town car. Even through his sunglasses, the California sun seemed excessively bright. Or maybe it was because of the pulsing in his head. Partway up the sidewalk, a car door slammed behind him.

"You can wait here," Beau called back to Warner. "I'll only be a few minutes."

"I'd like to come with you."

Beau stopped and turned around, curious. Warner didn't 'like' to do things Beau hadn't asked him to—or at least, he never expressed it. "Why?"

Warner shifted from one foot to the other. "The same reason you're here instead of just sending me to pick Brigitte up. For support."

Beau walked back until he was face to face with Warner. He removed his sunglasses to look him in the eye. "Don't think I haven't noticed your behavior the past few weeks."

Warner's spine straightened as if trying to meet Beau's height. "Sir?"

"Defending her behavior to me. Sticking your nose where it doesn't belong. I should've suspected earlier. You've always been the only one who can stand to listen to her babble senselessly for hours."

"If you're suggesting I'm in love with your sister," Warner said, hesitating only a moment, "you'd be right."

"How long?"

"Years."

Beau pulled at the knot around his neck. The sun was unforgiving today. "You should tell her that."

"I did." He glanced away briefly. "While you were away. I needed to distract her the night you left for Missouri. She wasn't doing well."

"She never does while I'm away." Beau sighed, nodding back toward the doctor's office. "Is that why we're here?"

Warner nodded. "She came to me after your argument. Nothing unusual there, except this time when she tried to call and beg you not to go after Lola, I put my foot down."

Beau frowned at Warner, his employee who exhibited less emotion than a robot. "And how did that go?"

"She'd told me what you'd said about me having feelings for her, so I said it was true. And I asked her why she wanted to be second in your eyes when she was first in mine."

Beau couldn't remember Brigitte ever responding to romantic gestures, though he suspected she didn't care to share them with him. He almost didn't want to ask. "What'd she say?"

"We had an honest talk. She was young when she moved here and hadn't dealt with losing her mother the way a young girl should. She replaced one family with another before she ever had a chance to feel anything."

Warner was always in the background, but Beau hadn't realized how closely he must've been paying attention to them over the years. "She's terrified I'll leave her too," Beau said, "and she'll end up alone."

"She won't, and I told her so. Said she's always had two people who would never abandon her, she just needs help seeing that."

Beau gave Warner a heartfelt nod. He was grateful, for once, to have someone else looking out for Brigitte's best interest. "Let's go inside."

They walked side by side to the therapist's office, where they sat in the waiting room. Beau had nothing else to say to Warner. He kept quiet, wiped sweat from his temple with his shoulder sleeve.

His phone broke the silence, but he checked the screen and put it back in his pocket.

"You can take it," Warner said. "We have a few minutes."

Beau glanced at him and leaned his elbows on his knees. "It's fine." It rang again and didn't stop until Beau finally answered it. "What is it?"

"What do Texas, New Mexico and Arizona have in common?" Detective Bragg asked, sounding more joyful than Beau thought possible.

"A lot, actually," Beau said.

"They're all on the way back to Los Angeles. She should be on our turf by tomorrow."

Beau looked at the ground, bouncing his knee up and down. He'd learned his lesson—finally—when it came to assuming anything about Lola. Yet the promise he'd made himself to walk away was tenuous, something that could easily be broken if he wasn't careful. A memory nagged at him—*Texas, New Mexico, Arizona*—but he shook his head quickly to deflect it.

"You hear what I said?" Bragg continued. "She's coming home."

That was a blow. Lola might be coming back to California, but if she considered Beau her home, she wouldn't have left him this way. He massaged his forehead. "We decided to drop this."

"That was before I knew we were at the end."

"You were right, though. She wants to be…" It wasn't a memory nagging him—it was his dream from the airplane. The details were fuzzy, but he could clearly picture Lola in the desert with their daughter. He stilled his leg. "Did you say Arizona?"

"Got a pending motel charge in Tucson just now. That's why I called."

The doctor's office door opened, and a woman spoke. "See you in a few days, Brigitte?"

"I have to go," Beau said, pulling his phone away.

"Maybe I was wrong." Bragg cleared his throat. "About her not wanting to be found. Maybe I had it wrong."

Beau didn't think it could be that simple. "Congratulations on your second retirement, Bragg.

Thanks for all your help."

He hung up the phone as Brigitte entered the waiting room and stopped when she saw them. She turned a balled-up tissue over in her hand, a watery smile on her face. "You both came."

Beau stood, and she went directly to him. She hugged him, melting against his body only a second before she pulled back. She narrowed her red-rimmed eyes. "You've been drinking."

"Not yet."

She shook her head. "Then you're wildly hungover."

"It's been a rough couple weeks."

Brigitte frowned, but for once it didn't alarm him, since it was purely concern. She looked about to speak but then closed her mouth. Beau had gotten off the airplane and had a voicemail from Brigitte—she was going into therapy, for real this time. Careful not to upset her, he hadn't yet mentioned any details about Lola or his trip, and Brigitte hadn't asked.

"Your big meeting with VenTech is tomorrow. Shouldn't you be at work prepping?"

Beau definitely should've been with his team, which was locked in a conference room surrounded by Subway sandwich wrappers. Things'd happened so quickly that the staff had been taking turns pulling all-nighters. Beau was having a hard time remembering why he needed VenTech so badly, though, and as a result, had been avoiding the office. That, and he was proud of Brigitte for finally making a good decision.

"I thought maybe my *soeurette* could use me more,"

he said. "And I wanted to congratulate you."

She shrugged. "It wasn't an easy decision, but with some urging from—"

"Not about that." He jerked his head fractionally in Warner's direction.

"Oh." She looked down between them, but it was hard to miss the pink flush of her pale skin. "I don't know where I was all these years. I must've been blinded by some—*thing.*"

Beau nodded that he understood. In her reality, she and Beau were linked for life. Whether it was simply familial for her or something more, Beau'd never asked, in case he didn't like the answer. Her fear of loneliness was strong enough to shut out the truth. Beau was fine being pushed aside so Warner could take his place.

"We'll have to figure out a new arrangement," Beau said, loud enough for Warner to hear. "I'm not having my sister's boyfriend drive me around."

"Fire me."

Beau and Brigitte both turned to him. She disengaged from Beau to go hug Warner instead. "But, Brandon, darling, you love what you do."

Beau made a face. *Brandon?* He looked between them, suppressing his reflex to stop them from touching. He'd practically pushed Brigitte into Warner's arms, but seeing them together would take some getting used to.

"I can always do it somewhere else," Warner said. "At the end of the day, it's just a job."

Any other time, Beau might've scoffed at that— just a job? What else was there? But since Lola had disappeared, what he'd missed most was having someone to look forward to all day. He'd promised to make her a priority, but then he'd look up from his computer at some point to see afternoon had become evening, and he still hadn't finished. That was a mistake he was paying for dearly in the tender of regret. Maybe if he'd chosen her over work, like Warner was with Brigitte, Lola would've found a reason to stay.

Beau tuned out his thoughts and focused on Brigitte, who was relaying her session to them.

"At first, it wasn't too bad, mostly discussing what'll happen over the course of my therapy. Then she asked about the accident, and…" She stepped away from Warner to take Beau's hands. "And we talked about you. Me and you."

Beau wasn't looking forward to hearing whatever she said next, but he remained still despite his instinct to flee.

She must've noticed, because she held his hands more tightly. "Do you need to hear this from me? The doctor says I should tell you." She looked into his eyes. "You're a good brother. If I ever made you think otherwise, I'm sorry."

He shook his head. "I just want to see you healthy and happy."

"I'm not your responsibility. You don't have to take care of me."

Brigitte, on her own two feet, without him to support her? He couldn't picture it. "It's the nature of our relationship."

"Sometimes it's okay to let me fail or fall on my

face. All I ask is that you're there to help me off the ground."

Beau had his complaints about Brigitte, and sometimes she made his life hard. But without her, who would he be? He didn't want to know, and he'd never wanted to be rid of her. Not completely, anyway. "I'm not going anywhere."

"I don't mean your money, Beau. Sometimes I just need you to be there when I call. That's the relationship I want us to have."

Beau's hands were clammy. He'd bent over backward his whole life to make sure Brigitte and his mom were comfortably set up, never without food, shelter or, of course, the finer things in life. "I thought we already had that."

"We don't. I've spent the last twenty years just trying to get your attention, but nobody has your attention like your money."

Lola had said the same thing in different words. With a sharp pain in his chest, Beau briefly wondered if this on top of everything else was finally just going to kill him.

"Don't be upset," Brigitte said. "*I* know it's how you show affection. But it wasn't enough for Lola, and it's not enough for me anymore. I need a different kind of support from you now."

"So, what—I'm the bad guy all the time? For everyone?"

"No. Since we were together when our parents died, I thought we were connected on some supernatural level. But maybe that's a load of shit—at

148

least, that's what the doctor seems to think. I've been a burden. You're not responsible for me—or your mom, for that matter. You're not the man of the house. We can't keep pulling you in different directions."

"I want to take care of both of you, but you guys make it difficult to do a good job."

"So don't do it anymore." She cleared her throat. "Take care of Lola instead."

Beau wanted his hands back, but Brigitte wouldn't let them go. "It's over," he said, subject closed, nothing else to say.

Brigitte looked down. "Ten years ago, you came home a complete mess because a *stripper* had turned down the money it'd taken you your whole life to earn. Remember that night?"

It was a rhetorical question. Of course Beau remembered every nuance of the hour he'd spent with Lola, the way his heart had stabbed with every footstep he'd taken on his way out of the club. "What about it?"

"Tell me what happened."

"You already know the story—inside and out."

"Just tell me."

Beau sighed, glancing back at Warner. He'd also heard the story, so there wasn't one reason to tell it. "I gave up a lot for my first website, so when it sold for millions, it was surreal. The night I signed the papers, I was on a high. After years of having no social life, no women, I wanted someone that night. A beautiful girl to celebrate with. I walked into that strip club, and—" Beau paused, remembering how Lola had glistened and glittered from her shiny, black hair to her diamond bikini. "And there was no more beautiful woman than her. But she wouldn't have me, because she knew what she was worth. I tried to buy her for a night, but she didn't have a price."

Brigitte stared up at him, silent until Beau got uncomfortable. "What?" he asked.

With a disbelieving shake of her head, she said, "I've just never heard you tell it that way. It was always about what she'd done to you, or the pain she'd caused. You love her."

Beau took his hands away finally, wiping them on his slacks. "Not much I can do about it either way."

"What happened when you went to find her?"

"Nothing. Not a fucking thing." He shrugged. "By saying nothing, she's made herself clear."

"You're giving up?" She rushed the words out, bouncing once on the balls of her feet. She would have him all to herself again. "But you never give up on anything worth saving."

It took Beau a moment to register that she wasn't rooting against Lola. He cocked his head, glancing at Warner, whose lips were pressed together with a suppressed smile. "I'm not giving up. I figured it was time I start respecting her decision. Anyway, I wouldn't know where to find her."

Brigitte rolled her eyes as if the answer were obvious to everyone but Beau. "Stop acting like her opponent," she said, "and start thinking like her partner. What is she looking for? Where is she going to find it?"

Beau swallowed, looking away. Respect wasn't the only reason he had to let her go. Her name grated when he heard it aloud. He couldn't remember word for word the last thing she'd said to him. He would never tease her about seeing the ball of twine in person, as he hoped she had.

"We should go," he said, turning away from their raised eyebrows and craned necks.

Warner went by Brigitte's apartment first and walked her to the door. Beau watched them interact without a third party. When Warner leaned in to kiss her, she almost shied away. Warner wiped his forehead with the back of his hand. Beau doubted he and Warner suffered from the same kind of sweat, though. Beau looked out the other window to give them privacy.

"You never give up on anything worth saving."

"Stop acting like her opponent, and start thinking like her partner."

Beau asked himself when he'd ever *not* fought for anything in his life. Everything he owned, he had because he'd fought for it. He'd even fought *himself* countless times. He was tired. Thirty-seven years he'd been fighting without a break and carrying at least one person on his back. He looked at his watch, wondering how much longer he'd have to wait for a drink.

◆ ◆ ◆

Warner glanced at Beau in the rearview mirror for the third time in ten minutes. Beau'd insisted he'd take a taxi so Warner could stay with Brigitte, but Warner wouldn't have it. He pulled up to the curb in front of Beau's house and left the car idling.

Warner had been with Beau ten years. Their relationship had worked itself into a groove long ago. Beau took a stab at what was bothering Warner. "Should we discuss our new arrangement?"

"No need, sir. I'll start looking for a new employer in the morning."

Beau studied him. He seemed to have no problem making such a drastic change. Apparently, everyone around Beau was moving on, working toward becoming better people. "Let me do it," Beau said. "I only want you working for the best."

"Thank you, sir."

"You don't need to call me sir anymore."

Warner nodded once. "All right."

Beau hesitated. "About Brigitte. Do you think the counseling will help?"

"Yes. She's tried before, but this time, she actually wants things to change."

Beau hoped that was true. She certainly had never sought help on her own without Beau pushing her. "Good." Beau reached for the handle.

"It may be selfish," Warner continued, "but I hope she doesn't change much. I want her to get better and somehow stay the same. Does that make sense?" He chuckled to himself, shaking his head. "She's a handful, but she grows on you."

Beau released the door and sat back in his seat. He smiled a little. "Just be careful what you wish for. Brigitte might mellow a bit, but her fire never burns out. No matter how many times I've wished it would."

"Better or worse, that fire's what I love about her,"

Warner said.

Beau looked at the floor. *Fire.* He missed Lola's fire most of all. The way she screamed at him, fought him, submitted to him, came for him, challenged him. *Fuck.* He needed a drink immediately before he lost it.

"Sir?" Warner asked. "Beau?"

Beau looked up. "Yes?"

Warner turned in his seat to look at him, went to speak. He shut his mouth, looking thoughtful. "I've been there from the beginning. That first night you picked Lola up at her house. I see how you are about her. I just—well, I know it hasn't been…if you need to talk—"

Beau held up his hand. "Not now. Definitely not now. Go home, Warner."

"Yes, sir."

Beau got out of the car, went inside and veered directly for his study. He poured himself a drink and took a sip. The burn was a poor substitute for Lola, but it was as close as he could get.

Brigitte wanted Beau to put himself in Lola's shoes. He was already in them, though, whether he wanted to be or not. He now knew the pain he'd caused her and understood how it'd driven her away. The question was why she was coming home. She had the money and motive to stay hidden. Maybe she thought Beau had given up on her. Or maybe she wasn't returning to Los Angeles at all.

Beau, a man who lived life on the top floor of whatever building he was in, had never felt smaller or more insignificant. Without Lola by his side, he was nothing. She'd left a hole in her place that'd grown into a canyon each day she was missing. Had she felt the same that morning she'd left his hotel room? Was she still lost and confused, or had she found her way?

It'd been years since Beau had encountered a problem he couldn't buy his way out of. Once she was back in California, he could spend every dollar he had to track her down. He could fill her space with flowers or show up in a helicopter and take her to Paris for a night. He could build her a place to dance to her heart's content. Money was the only way he knew how to prove how much he loved her, but it wasn't right. Lola didn't deserve to be bought—he knew that better than anyone. He should've known that from the start.

She deserved a man who would fight for her. Lay down his life for her. Who would earn her love, no matter what it took, because he couldn't survive another day without it. A man who could give her the things money couldn't buy. Finally, Beau understood—he was that man. And he knew where she was headed.

Chapter Seventeen

Arizona had stretched-cotton clouds, blue skies and long-fingered cacti. Lola stuck her left arm out the window, opening her hand against the dry, mild air. It was cooler now that she'd passed Phoenix, and the desert was changing from sand to brittle grass, shrubs and trees.

She'd reached Tucson thinking it would be the last night of her road trip. Los Angeles was only seven or eight hours from there. But in the motel the night before, she'd lain on a hard-mattress bed, staring up at a dark ceiling, insomnia an overzealous friend. She didn't even know where she'd stop and park her car once she got home. That thought'd made her body heavy on the bed, as if she might risk driving right through the city if she didn't figure it out soon.

Back when she'd had nothing to lose, it'd been easy to slide behind the bar of Hey Joe. To insert herself into Johnny's life one toiletry at a time. To slip beside him in his bed. Things weren't so clear now. She only knew what she didn't want for herself or her baby—a life where things happened to her. She was capable of taking charge now. That was what she'd gained by choosing herself and driving away from something she loved.

She'd lain awake most of the night, memories of Beau gum-stuck to her no matter how hard she tried to clean them away. How he focused when he shaved. He didn't make coffee for himself, but he liked to leave her a fresh pot on the mornings he didn't see her, his version of a love note on his pillow. It was always too strong, the coffee. But what she remembered as clearly as those little things was the waiting. For the end. For him to come home. If Lola wasn't the woman Beau would leave work early for, then one didn't exist. By now, he would know it too, what he'd given up to stay on top.

Sometimes, though, he'd tried to make it right— most notably the evening they'd had coffee in his den and talked until the near dawn. After replaying that night's conversation about travel, she'd decided there'd be one more stop on her trip. It would be a way to pay homage to her time with Beau—and a place to seek answers. The earth had bottomed out from under her, but she was climbing her way back up. Where better to end this trip than a rift so deep, it could never be repaired?

Lola arrived at the Grand Canyon in the late afternoon. She waited in a line of cars to pay the entrance fee. The only money she carried now was a couple hundred dollars divided between her wallet and her suitcase. The rest was in a bank where it belonged. She passed through the cabin-esque, log-walled entrance, and drove to the parking lots. She circled them for fifteen minutes, hitting her brakes now and then for tourists in bunched-up socks and cameras around their necks. Everybody was arriving. Nobody seemed to be leaving.

Finally, she parked and got out, stretching her arms. The clear, cool sky was stark against its russet surroundings. A bus stopped at the curb of the Visitor's Center and a group spilled out. They wore more layers than she did and talked loudly about the impending sunset. She shoved her hands in her hoodie pockets and tried to weave through people, but they kept stopping to take pictures before they'd even made it to the canyon. She looped wide around the swarm. What she wouldn't miss about traveling was the crowds, lines, limited parking. People on top of people at every attraction.

She stopped first at the busiest spot, a fenced overlook. She leaned on a railing, gazing into the mouth of the canyon, wide open and the color of a bruise. It gave her a thrill. She scanned the canyon walls, a rust-rainbow of beiges that morphed into earthy purples and pinks as the sun lowered.

A man asked her to move out of a picture he was taking of his wife. Lola left to find a more secluded spot, her tennis shoes crunching along the path. Only Mather Point, where she'd just stood, was enclosed. The rest was open, the canyon ready to swallow anyone who might misstep. She walked the rim, the crowd thinning, and spotted a cliff where she could be alone.

She climbed off the path, down between two boulders. A whitewashed rock jutted out into the canyon and came to a square point. The thought of standing on the edge made her heart skip, but she hadn't come all this way to live life in the curtains. With slow, careful steps, she walked to the ledge. It was a straight drop down. Being so far up was physical, her stomach and legs prickling like being stabbed by hundreds of tiny pins. As a teenager, she'd get high trying to feel something akin to this. She shivered with a breeze, the hair on the back of her neck waking up.

"I'm ready for some answers," she said out loud, her words expanding into nothing. She felt, inside, like the valley—deep, dangerous, beautiful. She had no idea how to be a mother. She didn't take it lightly, that responsibility, and it scared her. She needed to know how one night could've led to all this. One night, she'd looked over her shoulder and found Beau. One night, they hadn't used protection. "I don't know if I can do this by myself."

Nothing happened. The canyon was still. She wasn't going to find answers here. They were inside her, but they'd only come with time. She closed her eyes to take a mental picture, the wind light in her hair. She told herself she wasn't alone, that as much as it'd been forced on her, she'd also chosen this path. She wouldn't have been happy in that life with Beau, never having healed that wound he'd left, always being second place to his money.

That was where she stood, alone but steeped in

hard-won peace, when he spoke from behind her.

"So this is where it ends."

Chapter Eighteen

Lola opened her eyes abruptly, her peacefulness shattering. Beau was so unexpected that her heart doubled in size and speed, fat and swollen, clambering up into her throat like a live fish trying to escape. She knew that voice, that unforgiving tone, as surely as she knew what would happen if she were to take one step forward.

"Turn the fuck around," Beau said.

The deeply-orange sun crested from behind a cloud, blinding her. She turned her head to the side, Beau in her peripheral vision. Closer than he should be. There was no one person she wanted to see least and most in that moment. She didn't want to explain herself, but she needed him to understand.

"Look me in the eye," he said. "You owe me that much."

She couldn't bring herself to do it. It was bad timing, being so close to the edge, vulnerable and unprepared for him. This wasn't on her terms like it was supposed to be.

But with the gravelly chew of his shoes, she turned quickly. She shielded her eyes, his shadow black and nebulous, blinking away the sun's neon imprint. "Wait," she said.

He'd already stopped, his feet apart, almost aggressively so. It reminded her of the beginning, the way he'd stood that first night on the Sunset Strip sidewalk, intruding on her moment alone. Just like then, he was perfectly put together in his suit, his dress shirt tucked in, his navy tie straight. Only his pants were wrinkled across the front, as if he'd been sitting in them for a long time. The day's last light illuminated his brown hair gold.

"What are you doing here?" she asked.

"What am *I*...?" He paused, running his hands up the sides of his nose. He inhaled a deep breath, made a fist, jammed a rigid finger into his chest. "You're asking me why *I'm* here? I'm doing the same thing I did in L.A., Missouri, New Orleans. I'm goddamn looking for you."

Lola wished for something to steady herself on—a gate, a fence, even a tall boulder. She checked over her shoulder—nothing but white-rock ledge. She pulled her shoulders up as she looked back at him. "I never asked you to do that."

"You turned my life upside down." He scrubbed his whiskered chin and shoved a hand in his hair, ruining it. It was too long and not as perfect as she'd thought. "More than once. Did you think I'd lie down and take that? You didn't think I'd fight back?" He'd said *fight* angrily, with a hard "F" and clipped "T".

Lola's heart beat a mile a minute, the tips of her fingers and toes tingling. "I don't want to fight with you, Beau," she said calmly. "I don't want to play. I just want the bullshit to end."

"It's over," Beau said. "Believe me. This game ended a long time ago."

"Then why are you here?"

"I think I'll ask the fucking questions, thank you." He took a step forward, and Lola instinctively moved back a little. "What happened to you that night?"

"I did what I had to do." She leveled her eyes on him. "What you *made* me do. You really thought I could love you after what you did to me?"

"Don't pretend you're innocent here, Lola." His nostrils flared. "Or do you go by Melody now?"

She kept her arms straight at her sides, caught off guard to hear her real name from his mouth. She hadn't thought he would remember that detail from the VIP room. "Is that how you found me?"

"That and a lot of money."

Her jaw tingled, saliva pooling in her mouth. She didn't know what answer she'd expected or hoped for with him. "Of course. Money."

"At first, yes," he continued. "But it only got me so far. After that, I had to figure it out on my own." He squinted, holding his arms out, nodding. "I'm a little late, but I made it. Not bad considering you left me with nothing to go on."

His words were bitter like his tone. He grabbed the

knot of his tie and loosened it, leaving it crooked. There wasn't even a sliver of relief or happiness in his eyes.

Lola swallowed. "What are you going to do to me?"

"I've been asking myself the same thing." He took another step.

"I can't go through this again," she pleaded, shaking her head hard. "I've made peace with the pain."

"I haven't."

Lola glanced around without turning her head from him. There were only two exits from this situation—forward or backward.

"What was it all about?" he asked. "I want the truth, so help me God. Don't bullshit me."

Lola opened her mouth, but nothing came. How could she explain what it'd been like to finally give in to her love for him after fighting it so hard, only to have him break her big, happy heart in half? And then—to have to pretend to worship him for weeks as she nursed her wounds in private? *That* was bullshit.

"That night," Lola started.

He jerked his head to the side. "Which one?"

"In your hotel room, when we were planning how to leave Johnny. I'd never—it was the most—" Lola wiped her palms on the seat of her jeans. "You didn't ask. You just took. All of it. All of me."

"But you came back. You gave me another chance, and I did my best to make up for—"

"I *loved* you," she said, the word dropping like an axe between them.

They stood there a moment, two actors on an open

164

stage, leaves rustling, voices distant, temperature dropping. A train horn echoed through the canyon.

"You don't anymore?" he asked.

Lola looked down at the ground. What did it say about her that she still loved him after everything he'd put her through? Through all the lies, the spite, the games—her heart ached for him when he was right in front of her the same way it had when he was half a country away.

She looked up, keeping strength in her face, even though her body had begun to tremble. "My love hasn't gone anywhere. It's still in the garbage where you left it."

"I knew I was making a mistake that night. Even while I was doing it. But I'd gotten in too deep to pull myself out. Was it not enough punishment that I had to live with that? Knowing I loved you, but I could never truly make up for how badly I'd hurt you?"

"Knowing is one thing. You deserved—*deserve* to live the depth of your mistake."

"For how long?"

"That's for you to decide." She shrugged, limp and unconvincing. "It isn't something your assistant can add to your calendar. My forgiveness doesn't matter—you need your own."

"Where do you get off telling me what I need? Patronizing me? You have no idea what I've been through."

She shuffled back the last few inches, glancing behind her again. "Yes, I—"

"You don't know. You didn't care to," Beau

165

continued, another step. "And I still have nothing. I don't know where you went from Cat Shoppe. How you got there. Why. If you laid beside me in my own bed, plotting against me."

Her throat thickened. She didn't respond. It didn't look as though he expected her to. He was in front of her now, and she was cornered. She dug her heels into the sand. If she screamed, would anyone hear? Would it even matter? Nobody was close enough to get to her in time. All she'd done was even the score. But maybe Beau didn't see it that way. Maybe to him, she had a debt that was too great to pay.

He reached up. "Even with all that—"

"Stop." Her heart hammered. She squeezed her eyes shut. Everything on her body was rigid except for her arms, curved gently over her stomach. "I'm p—"

"I forgive you," he said. "I forgive myself. And I surrender."

Her body shook, her breath stuttering out of her mouth, wispy little butterflies. She balled a hand at her chin over her mouth, surprised to find it wet. She hadn't realized she'd been crying.

When she opened her eyes, his arms were spread as if to say it was all he had. She couldn't see anything but him and his hawk-like wingspan.

"I don't know if that's what you wanted, Lola, but you win."

Her chest deflated, relief and regret seeping through her. Surrender, forgiveness, victory. What was even left to win? What kind of prize was this to have fought so hard for? She shook her head. "That's not why I left."

"Then why?" He dropped his arms at his sides, his expression earnest, his thick eyebrows heavy in a different way than they just had been. "To escape? Or to get me to see?"

She shifted on her feet. "To see what?"

"I was stupid for you. You and I went deeper than anything, and I fought back out of fear. But I'm done making that mistake. My weapons are at my feet."

She waited, but he didn't continue. He hadn't moved back even an inch.

"That's it?" she asked. "That's your apology?"

"I'm sorry I hurt you. But I don't regret it. We wouldn't be here if I hadn't."

"Here?" Her hands still trembled. She closed them into two fists. "*This* is a good place to you?"

"It's where I should've been from the start. It was hell not knowing where you were. It opened my eyes, though, Lola. And like I said, now I finally see."

Lola tried to shut the words out. She believed him—tormenting him with her absence was the purpose of her plan. But his surrender wasn't, and it felt better than it should to hear he wasn't finished with her yet. "We both set out to destroy each other," she said. "How do I know that isn't what you're doing now?"

"Trust. Neither of us is good at it, but we each need it now. You know I love you—it's not a question of that. It's a question of if you'll let me. I do…love you."

She paused. It didn't shock her, but as his words registered, she realized that no matter how strongly she knew it in her gut, she'd thought she'd never hear him tell her he loved her. And that she'd somehow be okay with that. "I know you do. I always knew. You were the one who didn't."

"I do now. I get it. Put an end to this, Lola. I've repented. I've suffered. For you."

"How do I know? I wasn't there. I didn't see any of it."

"You chose not to. At least I looked you in the eye when I hurt you."

Her cheeks flushed. She wanted to be the only one who was justifiably angry, but he was right—and it embarrassed her. "So what? That makes it better?"

"There's no 'better' in this situation. We learn from our mistakes and move forward. I'm here to bring you home. To get the light back in my life."

The sun disappeared behind the rocky horizon. Lola had goose bumps everywhere and sweat along her hairline. These were things she thought she'd never hear. She jutted her palms between them. "Can you just step back? This is making me nervous."

He took her by the arm, his hand warm through her jacket, and pulled her closer to him.

Lola shrugged him off. "Not just the cliff."

He took some steps away without turning his back to her. In their relationship, she'd always been the one out on a ledge, expected to trust him blindly. To get into a stranger's limo, to uproot her life based on two nights.

"I've had a lot of time to think," Lola said, off the overhang now. "A lot of time alone. I came here for answers because…you said you got them here."

"Did you get them?"

She stuck a hand in her pocket, picked at some lint. "No."

"I never said I got answers, Lola. I said I came here looking for them. I don't like it here. It's so fucking bottomless, it just makes me feel like I have no control at all. But what I did get here was perspective. And I'm glad those answers never came, because it taught me a valuable lesson. Only one person makes things happen in my life."

"You."

He nodded. "So that's why I'm here. To do what it takes to fix this."

She lifted her chin. "I got some answers, Beau, just not here. This is my life, and I decide. You don't get to come here and tell me my trip is over and we're back together."

"I understand, but—"

"Don't interrupt me. I'm not going to make the same mistakes I did with Johnny."

Beau reeled back. "What's that supposed to mean?"

"I'm not coming back to L.A. because *you* say it's time. I'll do it when I decide it's right for me."

He worked his jaw side to side a moment. "I've told you repeatedly, I'm not Johnny. Your happiness is my priority, and from now on, that's what drives my decisions. I'm here to take you home because I believe it's in your best interest."

"Why is it always what you say?" she asked, her voice rising. "When do *I* get to decide?"

He showed her his palms. "We're a team. You

169

never have to be anything other than you when you're with me. You said it yourself that first night—I didn't choose you because I was looking for someone to roll over and take it."

Beau had always wanted Lola as she was—as long as it was on his terms. She shook her head, still uncomfortably close to the ledge. "It's not enough."

There was struggle in his face, his eyes, when he said, "It was once."

She nodded, remembering. *"I want you to know—to me, you are enough..."*

"I'm talking about all this." She gestured around them. "You can't just ask me to forgive you because you realize the mistakes you've made."

Beau inclined his head a little, squinting at her. "So what're you saying? This is just done?"

"Why'd you come here?"

"I couldn't walk away without knowing I'd tried."

"You tried, I'll give you that. But this is where it ends," she repeated his words back to him.

He shook his head. "I was talking about the torment, the pain, the games. All of that ends now." He gestured between them. "Not this."

Lola looked at Beau. He *was* trying, but she needed more. She needed all of him the way she'd been prepared to give him all of herself. He had to be exhausted by his love for her, because their child deserved that from both of them.

"This. Us," Lola said. "This is where *we* end."

"Don't." He shook his head. "You can't tell me you drove all that time and never thought of me. Never wished to be back in my arms, to be loved by me. That you—"

"You have no idea—"

"That you don't still love me—"

"Of course I do," Lola cried. Late nights clutching her pillow, wishing it was *him*. Driving for hours trying to think of anything but *him*. It wasn't fair that even when she hurt him, she hurt herself. She never got a break from the pain, and he had the nerve to come here and accuse her of otherwise. "You don't think this has been torture for me too? I fucking loved you with everything. You could've burned every last dollar—I wouldn't have cared. I loved the way you loved me, something nobody ever gave me. Fuck you," she said, reluctant tears flooding her eyes, "for thinking you suffered more than me."

"I broke your heart—fine. Mine broke every day I woke up and thought, 'Today I'll find her. Today I'll bring her home.' Now I have you—and you're going to tell me no?"

"You deserved everything you got."

"I did. I accept that. But don't keep punishing me."

"You don't even know what lies ahead," Lola said and resisted touching her stomach again. If there was an ounce of love in him for her, she could tear his heart out every day once he found out she was pregnant. But she'd be tearing her own heart out too and now, she actually needed it to raise this baby.

"I don't deserve this anymore," he said.

"You deserve it," she snapped. She breathed hard, curling her hands in and out of fists. She'd been holding the reins for weeks, and she didn't know how to loosen her grip. "You deserve all of it. For being a monster."

"I've learned my lesson. And I'm grateful for that, because now I know I can make you happy. You're more than enough, Lola—the money doesn't mean shit if you aren't by my side. I want to try to be enough for you."

"No. You had your chance, and you blew it. We're finished, and there isn't anything you can say to change my mind."

Slowly, he inclined his head forward. "You're serious about this?"

"I will not make the same mistakes again."

They stared at each other, him looking on the verge of speaking until he closed his mouth. "I don't know how else to get you to see—I thought…I thought—"

"You thought what? You'd never have to pay for treating people like this?"

He looked away from her, his eyes eventually drifting down to the ground. He blinked, his hand twitched. His eyebrows lowered. And she watched his every move, not knowing what she was hoping for, just that he wasn't giving it to her. He turned around.

"Where are you going?" Lola asked.

He stopped, looked back. "I don't know. I'm standing here, prepared to do whatever you ask, but you're asking me to do nothing."

"No," she said sharply. She jabbed a finger in his direction. "*You* don't get to walk away. I do."

His eyebrows knit as he faced her again. "What?"

"Do you know how it feels to lay it all on the line

only to have the person you love tear you apart?"

He nodded. "I do now."

"No, you don't. You said you loved me—but *I* was about to give you *everything* I had. You waited until I was at my most vulnerable to rip my heart out. I want to do the same to you, and then *I* get to walk away. Do you understand?"

"No. I—"

"I want to gut you of your dignity."

His face went smooth, his body still. Dignity, pride, ego, his and hers—that was how they'd gotten here. Neither of them wanted to give up those things. "I don't know what else to say." Beau's jaw clenched as he swallowed. "I love you. I want to make a life with you. That's my everything."

"Stand on the cliff," she said. "You stand there for once."

He glanced behind her. "What?"

She looked back at that enormous hole in the earth and pointed at the crag. "You need to know how it feels to be cornered for once. To have no control."

He put his hands in his pockets and walked toward her without hesitating. She held her breath as they passed each other and only let it go once they'd switched spots. He walked over to the ledge and looked down, but only for a brief second. He turned his back to it. "I never thought I could love anyone the way I love you."

"Did you hear that in a movie?" Lola asked.

He narrowed his eyes on her, rolling his lips inward. "It's true, Lola."

"It's not good enough."

"I don't understand. What do you want from me?"

"I want you to give me what I gave you. Every last thing you have. And when you're emptied out, and your heart is in the dirt? I'm going to walk away, Beau. I'm going to leave you standing here in your own mess. You will never see me again. So, come on. If you love me like you say, you'll give me the closure I deserve."

He stared at her, something miserable in his green eyes. It was almost enough to get her to call this off, but this was what she needed. Because nobody could hurt Beau's pride worse than himself. If he could go to that place for her, knowing it wouldn't win him anything in the end, then maybe Lola could trust in what he was trying to tell her.

She held her breath, waiting. He made no move to speak, just blinked a few times. For a minute, she thought he couldn't do it. He couldn't give himself up to save them.

He inhaled deeply through his nose. "I already told you I love you. How am I supposed to explain how deep it goes?"

"Try." Lola turned sideways. "If you can't, you can leave."

He continued to look at her, finally shaking his head. "I thought I'd find you here after weeks of confusion, and finally all my questions would be answered. I knew we would fight. It's part of who we are, what we did to each other. We're both so angry. But I was going to take everything you had to give, and never once did I think that wouldn't be enough. In my gut, I knew—we'd leave here together."

"Both those nights, you let me live in a fantasy I thought was reality. Now it's your turn. Tell me all the details of this life you thought we would have. Where would we have gone from here?"

His hands strained in his pockets. It was ridiculous to see a man in a suit at a place like this, but it was his armor. His tie was still off center. "Don't make me do this," he said quietly.

She had done it, over and over, and in her experience—he had to know what he was losing in order to feel the full impact of its void. "Your plan was to come here and drive me off into the sunset? That isn't life," she said sharply. "Do it or leave. Go back to L.A."

"Back to L.A.," he repeated fast and loud, visibly tensing as though steeling himself. "That's where I would've taken you. Home, to the house—"

"I hated it there." It'd never felt like she'd belonged amongst the white carpets and polished wood. "That wasn't my home."

"Okay. I didn't know that," he said cautiously, grimacing. "So, then, I'd ask if you wanted to move to a different neighborhood, or if you'd found somewhere on your trip you liked better than L.A."

"You can't leave L.A."

He looked to the side, his eyebrows heavy, wrestling with something. "I could. It's not home anymore," he said distantly. "You are. Were."

Lola shifted on her feet. Beau was dedicated to that city even more than she was. "What about Bolt

Ventures?"

"I would've given it up. Or worked remotely. Or started something new. At the end of the day, it's just a job." He smiled a little as he said it, like he was sharing an inside joke. But he looked back at her quickly, serious again. "I would've come home at five. I don't want to spend another evening without you. I hate it. I hate coming home to an empty house. Before, I didn't know the difference, but I do now. It's excruciating."

Lola's blood rushed loudly in her head. As angry as she was, she recognized his breakthrough for what it was. He was giving her the control by living out this dream he'd never get, by making himself vulnerable. While she'd been gone, getting her back had still been a possibility in his mind. But now, he knew no matter what he said, she was going to leave. He didn't have to say anything. He could walk away.

"I love you," he said. "So much that I went to see your mom. Once, to see if she knew where you were. Then again—yesterday morning, on my way to work. I stopped and spent an hour there, having coffee, talking to her whenever there was a lull between tables."

Lola leaned in as if she'd misheard him. She hadn't known about the second time, since it was after she'd spoken to Dina on the phone. "Did my mom tell you where to find me?"

"No. I didn't even ask."

"Then why'd you go?"

He shrugged one shoulder. "I missed you so fucking much, I didn't know what to do. I couldn't go to Hey Joe. My own home is hell, the stupidest shit reminds me of you. She was the only real connection I had left to you."

Lola tried to focus, but her mind had latched onto this one little thing—he hadn't just gone to see her mom. He'd taken an hour out of his workday to do it. And it wasn't to get anything or manipulate anyone. It was only to feel close to Lola. And she realized they were standing at the Grand Canyon at five-thirty on a Tuesday, when he should've been fifty stories above Los Angeles, ruling his empire.

Her heart squeezed. She'd needed that from him even more than she'd realized. And his words reverberated inside her—*'I missed you so fucking much. I missed you so fucking much.'*

"Beau—"

"I canceled a meeting to be here," he continued. "Not just any meeting—it was with VenTech."

Lola tilted her head, the name vaguely familiar.

"The company that bought my first website and made me a millionaire. It's struggling to stay afloat. Today, ten years after they destroyed all my hard work for my competitor's benefit, Bolt Ventures was going to make an embarrassingly low offer to acquire VenTech. Just so I could say I told you so as I sold it off in parts."

Lola touched her throat. So she wasn't the only other one Beau thought deserving of his wrath. She had to know, for her own sake, if he could still be that vindictive. "Tell me you aren't going through with it."

"I was. This morning would've been my first time facing the founder since I'd signed the contract at twenty-seven. But because there was the smallest chance

177

I'd find you here today, I called off the deal last night. It wasn't worth it. None of this seems worth it anymore."

He'd been where she had, trying to find her, when he'd needed to be elsewhere. When he could've sent someone in his place. She'd been running away, living her life, and she'd also been his priority. And, like she'd planned all along, he'd learned his lesson. Canceling the acquisition was proof.

"Beau—"

"Wait. Before you go. I'm not finished." He doubled over, put his hands on his knees and took a deep breath as he stared at the ground. "I can't look at you for this part. I fucked things up, I know. But I had no idea how much I was throwing away. The reason I built all this, why I missed your dinners, was to make sure my family, whenever they came along, would have everything. It scares the fuck out of me to say this, but I thought that family would be with you, and I thought I'd worked hard enough, done enough, to deserve that." He squatted down, ran his hands over his face and looked up at her. "You're going to be a great mother, Lola. I've seen it."

She took two steps back, her hand on her stomach. There was only one way he could know about the baby. Dina's loyalty was to Lola, though—she had no reason to tell him. But he was as certain as she'd ever seen him. "What?"

"I'd hoped I'd be the one to give you that. I didn't even know I wanted it until…it doesn't matter. Fuck. It haunts me that someday you'll be the mother of someone else's child. But I have to live with that. So don't worry—I will get everything I deserve."

Tears streamed down her cheeks. He was almost on his knees, his chest opened, bleeding for her. All that, and he didn't even know she was carrying his child yet. It was enough. She put one hand over her mouth and sobbed into it while reaching out to him with the other. "Come here," she said. "Come home."

Chapter Nineteen

Beau was sure he'd heard wrong. That his mind was playing tricks on him. It wouldn't be a stretch—him, finally losing his sanity here on this ledge while Lola watched. He'd driven, literally, to the ends of the earth. He'd waited eight hours at the park's entrance for that red sports car to pull up, doubting himself, watching, watching, watching.

But it was worth it if he'd heard her correctly. Lola was crying into one hand, her other one outstretched to him. *"Come here. Come home."*

He couldn't move. As if getting into that position, kneeling at her feet on the edge of a cliff, had broken all his joints. It wasn't the abyss behind him that scared him but the idea of going on after seeing what could've been. Life had opened up to him, presenting him with all its beauty—he'd found her, and now he could make things right. Love her, marry her, give them both the child he'd dreamed about.

How could he miss it so much, something he'd never had?

He didn't blame Lola for breaking him down to this. It was the first time in his life he'd surrendered to someone else. Even the first two nights he'd spent with her, he'd given her just enough for them both to fall in love. But this wasn't love. It was something closer to death. A part of him had to die for Lola to know he wasn't the man she thought he was.

Beau eased from squatting to sanding, still unsure what she was offering him. Condolence? Pity? Something more? "But you said you were walking away."

She shook her head, removing her dampened hand to wipe her eyes. "Maybe I should, but I can't. I left to hurt you, hoping you'd regret what you'd given up, and I thought that would be it. I never planned to end up here."

Beau waited. He wanted to ask her if that meant she wasn't going to leave him there on the brink of his demise, but he was afraid one word from him might ruin it all.

"I'm happy in L.A., but I want to leave that house," she said. "I don't care where we go, it just has to have at least two bedrooms."

He stared at her, his heart rate increasing, unsure he could trust his ears. It sounded like she was saying she'd come home with him, but he didn't think he could take it if he was wrong yet again. He didn't know exactly what she was asking for, but he didn't care. "Consider the house gone. Whatever you want."

"I resented you." She paused. "For putting work first. I should've said it, but that would've meant I cared, and I didn't want to care. But I do now, so I'm saying it."

He nodded. Since she'd left, even he'd resented his work for what it'd cost him. "Work will always be a part of my life. I can't walk away completely."

"I don't want you to. It's your passion, but—"

"But it's not my priority. Not anymore. I will make changes, not because I have to, but because I have a reason to."

"That's not all," she said, eyeing him warily.

"I know it's not, but put me out of my misery. Please. Does this mean you're giving me a chance to earn you back?"

She reached out to him again, and this time, he went without hesitation. Those nights he'd had no idea where she was or if she was okay, he'd gone nearly mad, needing her back in his arms, the only place she was truly safe. Before he could put his hands on her, though, she took him by the wrist. Her long fingers wrapped around him, warming his chilled skin. She guided his hand to her waist, setting it there without letting him go. "You have nothing to earn," she said, looking into his eyes. "I see on your face what you've been through. When we were together, I know you never lied to me, never faked how you felt. I can forgive what you did because now that I understand you, I understand what drove you there. That Beau never would've stood where you just stood and willingly ripped his own heart out. I trust you."

Beau trusted her too, and he didn't question it. Hurting him was her way of fighting back. And she always would, he expected that from her. He loved that about her. But from now on, they'd be on the same side. "It's all I could've asked for from you. Forgive me. Love me."

"No," she said softly, shaking her head. "It's not all."

She readjusted her grip on his wrist—her palm was sweating. He glanced down. His hand wasn't actually flattened on her waist but her lower abdomen.

"When you said—" She paused, and he looked back at her face. Her expression had changed, her lips rolled inward with a frown. Her furrowed eyebrows lined her forehead with wrinkles. "Sometimes things don't really happen the way you plan—" She blew out a sigh and laughed in a strange, jittery way. "Obviously."

Beau lengthened his spine. Her demeanor had suddenly flipped, and he didn't need that. He didn't need to have the rug pulled out from under him again. Just a minute ago, she'd shoved her hand in his chest, taken hold of his heart, forced him to say *mercy*. Now, she could barely look him in the eye.

"What's wrong?" Beau asked. "Whatever it is, you can tell me. Nothing's going to change my—"

"I'm pregnant."

Beau jerked his head forward, his mouth and eyes wide open. They were both shaking—her body, his head side to side. They'd fucked a lot during the two nights of their arrangement, over and over. Him coming inside her, needing to own her in the quickest, most irrefutable way possible. He gulped some air, closed his mouth. "You're what? With—with me?"

She bit her bottom lip. "Yes. *We* are pregnant. I know it's not—what happened was, when my purse was stolen, my birth control was in there. When I moved in, we had those rules—I didn't think we'd—"

Beau squeezed his eyes shut for a brief second. He could barely hear her over the ringing in his ears. He was grateful he'd stepped away from the cliff. It came back to him all at once, his moment of weakness, taking her from behind against the bathroom counter. It'd nearly driven her away. He hadn't understood why then. It'd never occurred to him to ask about birth control.

That little girl in his dream, clutching Lola's leg, both of them otherworldly, divine. That was going to be his *reality*? After all the wrong he'd done, he was going to have that pureness in his life, that picture of perfection?

She was still talking. "And I know I signed that agreement—"

It was awkward handling her that way. He pulled his hand off her stomach and held it up. "Stop."

She blinked, her blue eyes sparkling more than usual, red and shiny with tears. By her quivering chin, she was trying not to cry. "You're not saying anything."

Already, he felt out of control. That's what children were—just a clusterfuck of disarray and irrational behavior. They couldn't be reasoned with.

Not his little girl, though. She'd be an angel.

Beau breathed hard through his nose, his insides running amuck. No, not his little girl, who was going to be as loved and revered as her mother.

He looked down at Lola, whose expression had morphed from anxious to horrified.

"What?" he asked. "Are you afraid of my reaction?"

Her face tightened up along with her jaw, her shoulders. "No." The wetness in her eyes evaporated. "You want this baby, Beau Olivier. Whether you know it or not."

He couldn't help his chuckle, even if it did sound a bit stiff. "I know it."

She opened her mouth.

Beau didn't let her speak. He dropped to his knees and slid up her top to expose her stomach. He cocked his head, examining the flawless, porcelain skin, the utter flatness of her abs. He glanced up at her. "You're sure?"

She nodded, slow but exaggerated. "Since before I even took the test."

Beau blinked lazily, feeling like he'd downed an entire bottle of his finest Scotch. "It's a girl."

Lola reared back a little, but he didn't let go of her. Her loud and sudden scoff skittered into a disbelieving laugh. "*Excuse* me?"

He got up again, brushing off his knees. "It's a girl. I've seen her."

She wrinkled her nose, pulling her head back. "Okay. You've finally…snapped."

He held her gaze, trying to stay serious, but he gave in and grinned. "That's possible. But if this is insanity, I like it here. Fuck, do I like it."

Her smile became hopeful, her face upturned to him like he was her sun. He knew without a doubt—he would never forget the beauty of this moment.

"You do?" she asked.

He took her face in his hands, felt her cheeks, her hair, ran the pad of his thumb over her bottom lip. "Is this too good to be real? Did I die in a plane crash on the way back from New Orleans?"

She took one of his hands and kissed his palm. "I'm so sorry I hurt you. Let me make it better. This is real. This is how it's supposed to be." She laced her fingers with his, watching them with a look of fascination. "Except you have one detail wrong. It's minor, really."

"What's that?"

"We're having a boy."

He arched an eyebrow, glancing down between them and back at her. "It's too early for you to know that."

"Call it a mother's instinct."

"Oh, mother's instinct. Right." He couldn't wait another second—he leaned down and kissed her on the lips once, a second time. She tasted a certain way—a certain way he'd missed. "What should we name her?"

"Him."

"Her."

"I'm positive," she said.

"I've never been more sure of anything," he said.

187

"I guess we'll see then, won't we?"

How could she even doubt him? Did she have any idea who she was dealing with? Once he described the details of his dream—the soft black curls of his daughter's hair, her giggle-drunk smile—Lola would see. Beau never ignored his instinct. After all, that was how they'd gotten there, on a cliff, on the brink of their lives, as night fell over the Grand Canyon. He'd seen a girl on a stage under a spotlight, and he'd known. *That one. I won't stop until I have* her.

BOOKS IN THE

Explicitly Yours Series

LEARN MORE AT
JESSICAHAWKINS.NET/EYSERIES

TITLES BY
JESSICA HAWKINS

LEARN MORE AT JESSICAHAWKINS.NET/BOOKS

SLIP OF THE TONGUE
THE FIRST TASTE
YOURS TO BARE

THE CITYSCAPE SERIES
COME UNDONE
COME ALIVE
COME TOGETHER

EXPLICITLY YOURS SERIES
POSSESSION
DOMINATION
PROVOCATION
OBSESSION

STRICTLY OFF LIMITS

ABOUT THE AUTHOR

JESSICA HAWKINS grew up between the purple mountains and under the endless sun of Palm Springs, California. She studied international business at Arizona State University and has also lived in Costa Rica and New York City. To her, the most intriguing fiction is forbidden, and that's what you'll find in her stories. Currently, she resides wherever her head lands, which is often the unexpected (but warm) keyboard of her trusty MacBook.

CONNECT WITH JESSICA

Stay updated & join the
JESSICA HAWKINS Mailing List
www.JESSICAHAWKINS.net/mailing-list

www.amazon.com/author/jessicahawkins
www.facebook.com/jessicahawkinsauthor
twitter: @jess_hawk

CPSIA information can be obtained
at www.ICGtesting.com
Printed in the USA
LVHW040723231118
598036LV00001B/309/P